To Simon,

2023

June Storm

June Storm

(If overthinking was a book)

Ramona
Lee Soo-Jun

Action Lee

Hardback ISBN: 978-1-7392786-1-8

Book cover art by Paul Harrison
Proofreading by Jason Cheung

ramonaleesoojun.com
Action Lee

Dedicated

to all those who wonder if I'm writing about them, but are too lazy to read a book, so will probably never read this;
to those who've lost the fight and to those who won't quit the fight against addiction;
to women;
last, but not least, to Jason. Thank you for everything.

SOME SORT OF DISCLAIMER

I'm apologising in advance for my weird English at times.

For the past year, I've been pushing myself to write this story in two languages consecutively. Subsequently, I've tortured Jason by having him read through it all and tell me off.

We've finally come to the conclusion that no amount of proofreading would save this story. It's written in Ramonglish.

I've been thinking of dozens of ways to disguise my lack of native knowledge. I've now decided to embrace it.

Trying your best is not always enough, I know. But after all, it's the journey we'll always hold close to our hearts. Not the destination. Perhaps the journey deserves to be celebrated, too.

Here's to another step closer to the dream. For stories deserve to be told. No matter their shape or form. Here's to you, the reader — the only real reason this story and many others have been put into words.

- the author

CHAPTER ONE

New Year's Eve

We begin our story on a street by Covent Garden. A group of hungover friends accidentally collided with another ensemble of drunk friends. Both camps apologised to one another and went their separate ways. In their wake, Santo appeared in frame, standing in front of a crowded pub. He quickly approached his friend with open arms and a cigarette between his fingers, hugging her tightly. As Italians are known for.

If it's been a while since you've last seen someone, but they immediately make it feel like it was yesterday, you can be sure that you've found the real deal. Santo was that kind of guy. Tessa greeted him with a smile.

"Eeeee!" Santo shouted enthusiastically, holding her with excessive excitement.

Brandon, still with both hands in his pockets, sighed and waited for the right opportunity to introduce himself as Tessa's boyfriend.

Brandon doesn't need any exordium on the part of the author.

"Are you here for the fireworks?" Santo asked.

"Let's hope so. Didn't buy tickets." Tessa laughed, now slightly embarrassed. "We're trying to find a bridge where we can see the sky." she added, still tightly held in Santo's arms.

Santo then looked over her shoulder, noticing Brandon.

"Oh, you must be…"

"Brandon, her boyfriend!" he emphasised, wanting to officially make acquaintance with Santo.

“Happy New Year!” Santo exclaimed, ignoring his outstretched hand and jumping straight to his neck to give him a big hug. “Well, what can I say, good luck!” he added, tapping Brandon’s shoulder lightly, yet firmly. “They blocked all the bridges with a view.”

“We’ll manage.” Brandon forced a smile. The kind of smile one might give whilst trying to shake a cat off his sock.

Tessa took Brandon's arm and smiled at Santo.

"I'm glad to see you again, Santo. It’s been a while…”

“Oh, the pleasure is all mine. Enjoy the show!” he gazed at his wristwatch. “It's twenty minutes to midnight.”

"We should hurry in that case." she laughed.

“Oh, before you go!” Santo exclaimed, suddenly looking from left to right.

He then ran to a pot near the entrance to the nearby pub, plucking a flower. Returning immediately to Tessa, he placed it inside the front pocket of her winter coat.

“Happy New Year, Tessa!”

“Happy New Year.” she smiled.

Saluting militarily, Santo made his way back to where the crowd was loudest.

As the couple headed towards any bridge that wasn’t closed down, Brandon sighed again. It was a telltale clue that he had been calculating and thinking deeply before beginning to speak afresh.

"You know all these friends of yours." he ventured. “Who keep prowling around you and who you keep in the friendzone… they’re just waiting patiently until you’re alone again, before attacking!”

“Are you jealous?” she asked, stopping.

“I'm not. I'm just telling you what I’ve noticed. As a man.”

Tessa took the flower out of her pocket, looking at it with melancholy.

“Flowers are beautiful, you know.”

“It's not worth buying flowers. They die. I mean, the ones you hold in your hand are already dead.”

“Still, they're beautiful. I like flowers. Every woman likes flowers. And chocolate.”

“Chocolate’s junk!”

"You got only one life, Brandon! One New Year's Eve a year. One birthday a year. One Valentine's Day a year. Your girlfriend takes care of you 365 days a year. Buy her flowers at least once a year."

"I bought you wine on Valentine's Day!"

"And I paid for the whole shopping cart that day."

"Well, it was your turn to pay."

"True," she confirmed, arranging the little flower back into her coat's pocket.

"And to be exact, you only paid 50% of the purchases that night, because the previous round was 100% paid by me, which means again, that in fact I also paid only 50% of what we bought together."

"You're very romantic…!" she sighed.

"Hey, I took the bags home!"

"We took a cab that night because you were too lazy to walk."

"Ah, true." he laughed. "You're right."

"Unfortunately, I am." she agreed, ambling towards the nameless, rusty bridge.

Although it wasn't a cold day, Tessa felt as if the wind started getting cooler. Bypassers seemed happier. Everyone else seemed luckier.

"Valentine's Day was invented by Americans to make money." Brandon spoke, jumping up the first step of the bridge in front of Tessa, walking ahead by himself.

A couple walked up the stairs, bypassing Tessa.

"It's the same with all those shampoo commercials. It's American propaganda." Brandon continued, reaching the platform.

Tessa joined him.

"You sound like Marx. You can stop now."

"Like Marx?! Marx was an arsehole!"

"Precisely."

"What are you talking about?"

Brandon leaned against the railing of the bridge and Tessa joined him.

"And what do you always have against Americans?"

"I've no problem with them. I only show you facts and statistics."

"You don't like Americans."

"I never said that!" he raised his voice. "I study up and I deliver facts. I observe and report. As I mentioned my opinion of your former coworker, Santo. My opinion, as a man."

"Whether it is true or not, I chose to be here with you. And this is my answer. As a woman."

From behind the decrepit bridge, fireworks started colouring the sky. The two looked up.

"Looks like we won't see anything from here."

"Yeah." she concluded.

It didn't seem worth it to bring up her suggestion that they should have reserved a spot where the fun was. Not again anyway.

"Hey, at least we saved some money!" he rejoiced.

"Ten pounds. Amazing."

"Actually, twenty. It would've been your turn to pay!" he chuckled; proud of his own statement, like a rooster that has just found its yard again after wandering all day lost in a drain in the neighbour's plantation. "But yes, to be more precise, you would've paid your share of 50%, which would've been, in fact, ten pounds."

"Fascinating."

Fireworks exploded behind the building.

"Tessa." he began suddenly, touching her shoulder.

She, in turn, rested her elbow on the railing.

"Brandon…"

"You know, I've been thinking a lot about the two of us lately. About us, in general. And as you well know, we've been together for a while now. To be exact, eleven months."

Fireworks continued to crack behind the building. The sky was lit in green and red. No snowflakes. Not even a raindrop.

"I was thinking of asking you, what would you think if we had an open relationship from now on?"

"An open relationship?"

"Yes, you know. Let's both start seeing other people…"

"Are you breaking up with me?" Tessa asked, with a clear voice.

"No… no! I didn't say that! I just want to diversify… We might both make interesting discoveries."

Tessa looked at the illuminated building, blind to the explosions above her. She felt like the sky was falling and the ground beneath her was trying to swallow her altogether.

A group of strangers greeted them–lively, drunk, and perhaps a little high as well. Their festive spirit was clear as they bellowed

"Happy New Year!" into Tessa's eardrums. She hadn't shaken hands with so many strangers against her will in a long time. The sky was clear. Not a single raindrop in sight.

Tessa was definitely omitting a particular detail. She had a hunch. At that moment, the Universe had sent her the first signal, that nothing, had to be the same ever again.

●

"Wait! Wait! What exactly does he want to diversify?!" Ruby exclaimed, picking up her coffee cup to sip from it. "And what did you say?"

Ruby was one of those colleagues you could always count on. She didn't have her own life under control at all, and she was far from satisfied with anything she ended up doing. But that never stopped her from being ready to offer the most detailed personal advice to others. Some of it was effective, other bits less so. But what mattered most was her intention, which always came from the depths of her sincere and sometimes slightly paranoid little soul.

Tessa walked across the office kitchen towards Ruby, bringing her cup of chamomile tea with her. The tea should've calmed her nerves, but today it made her even more restless.

"I told him I didn't want to be just one of his options, so I broke up with him."

"That's the move, sister! Never, but never, give them the satisfaction of being the ones to dump you!" Ruby exclaimed, raising her index finger.

"Did I do the right thing…?" Tessa asked in a low voice.

"Um, listen to me," Ruby grabbed both of Tessa's hands. "You're prettier than him and you have a better situation than him."

"I work in a call centre." Tessa replied, straightening her back and pointing around herself.

"Okay. That doesn't change the fact that you're prettier than him. You understand?" Ruby continued, sipping noisily from her coffee, putting the cup back on the table. "Repeat after me: 'I'm more beautiful than him! I'll be more accomplished than he is!'"

Tessa laughed awkwardly, looking at her cup, where she could see some of her reflection in her tea.

"Repeat after me: 'I'm more beautiful than him!'"

"I'm more beautiful than he is." Tessa murmured.

"With more soul! 'I will be more accomplished than he is!'" exclaimed Ruby.

"I'll be more accomplished than he is!" Tessa raised her voice, feeling encouraged.

"What's going on here?" the company's only IT specialist, Joe, chimed in. As he never had any work to do, he was always on the lookout for the latest gossip, bringing his empty coffee cup with him.

"Tessa dumped Brandon."

"In fact, he left me." Tessa added, aware that she was the victim in this situation.

"Hey, hey! From now on, we'll no longer spread this information!" Ruby insisted, as it was important to her that we kept to the "optimal" version of events.

"Brandon? That bloke who always had a problem with Americans?" Joe asked, playing with his cup, pushing it from one palm to another.

"That Brandon." Tessa approved.

"He had a problem with Americans?" Ruby lifted an eyebrow while Joe took a seat at the table.

"He definitely had a problem with Americans! But wasn't he also a Republican?"

"I don't know what he was. It doesn't matter." Tessa sighed, her voice drained.

"He had an issue with Americans?" Ruby repeated, waiting for details.

"The reason he never bought me flowers and chocolate is that flowers die and chocolate is junk. And the whole Valentine's Day concept is invented by Americans to make money."

"You're not the superficial type, I know, I kno–" said Joe.

"But didn't you say back in February last year that he bought you a big rose bouquet?" Ruby asked, frowning.

"I lied."

"Oh." Ruby murmured, pursing her lips.

"Apparently, showering was also invented by the Americans, to sell shampoos."

"Okay. I think I've heard enough."

"And we're completely brainwashed into believing that we need to take a shower every day and wash our hair maybe twice a week."

"My English ears are bleeding." said Joe, wincing sympathetically.

"During Victorian times, people washed once a month and they were quite happy folks," said Tessa. "He was trying to implement it to be happy too."

"Tessa, stop it. I've heard enough."

"He doesn't know how to keep a door open. He doesn't know how to walk you home, walk you to a train station." Tessa exclaimed. "And all that money counting. My turn to pay, your turn to pay…! 50%… Ah, it's not actually 100%, which is actually 50% after all!"

Ruby and Joe exchanged glances without making a sound.

"But guess who he bought chocolate for her birthday! His mother!" Tessa exclaimed, with wide-open eyes.

"Classic." Ruby concluded.

"Ah, but there's a kind of chocolate he liked too. I bought it because he liked it, for unspecified reasons. The ones with jam in the middle."

"Oh."

"But I was only allowed to eat with restraint." Tessa added.

"But you paid 50% of that product anyway."

"Right." Tessa approved. "But I like to take the whole cake and eat it in one go. Which he thought was a waste."

"Where's the waste?" Joe asked, cocking his eyebrows.

"Because I didn't enjoy it properly! He said the faster I ate, the sooner I wanted to buy a new pack. And that was a waste of money."

"Uhm, okay…!" Joe murmured, scratching his chin.

"And he liked to hold the cake in his hand, gnawing on the surrounding chocolate and eat the jam from the middle at the end." Tessa explained, gesturing.

"Okay, my dear, enough!" Ruby said, taking a more serious stance.

"He didn't even let me eat my portion at my own pace! The portion I paid for, with my own money!"

"That's enough." Ruby sighed, holding her coffee firmly in her hand.

"He was certainly a Republican." Joe commented.

"Can you please stop it with the politics?" Ruby muttered to him. "Don't you have a coffee to drink or something?"

"Ah, no." he replied, looking at his cup. "I came for water. I'm detoxing today. I feel like I only want to drink water."

"And he said that hair conditioner is useless and that only hair oil works. Just because oil was better for his hair!" Tessa continued. "He also loved vinegar crisps."

"Stop humiliating yourself." Ruby sighed.

"And he said I was wasting money on a conditioner. But I like the conditioner I use!"

"Hear me out." Ruby then spoke to Tessa, taking her hand. "From now on, you eat as many cakes with jam in the middle as you want, and as fast as you want, without anyone telling you what to do. Also use as much hair conditioner as you want!"

"She's right. I'm divorced, and I know what I'm talking about. The guy was definitely dating someone else." said Joe.

"You think so?" Tessa murmured.

"Absolutely! I know what I'm saying, trust me."

"I should've figured it out. From the second date! When "Nothing's Gonna Stop Us Now" was on the radio and he was ashamed that I knew all the lyrics to the song. I should've realised by then that we had nothing in common."

"You don't need him!" Ruby repeated. "Say after me: 'I don't need him!'"

"I don't need him!" Tessa recited.

She smiled, regaining her courage. And then a momentary flicker of thought made her stand up.

"I know what I'm going to do!"

Torrential rain could suddenly be heard through the metal door that exited the kitchen. It felt less like London and more like a monsoon.

"What?"

"Ruby, I'll go out with other men. Maybe even Americans."

"Wait, what did I miss?" Joe intervened.

"That's not a bad idea!" Ruby sounded thrilled. "The American accent always excites me. Especially those men who sound like cowboys."

"I think you've watched too many old movies. Nobody talks like that anymore." said Joe.

"You shut up. Your London accent makes me sick if you ask me. You don't even know how to pronounce your words properly. Sometimes you speak and I don't understand a thing you're saying!" exclaimed Ruby.

"Oh, I think it's time for someone to go back where she came from!" Joe teased her.

"Really? Then you go answer my phone calls," she replied. "And I can fix our computers that never have issues anyway in your place."

"It's not just about repairing computers."

"Whatever, the stuff that you're doing all day."

"I'm going to look for an American! I don't need Brandon!" Tessa decided to take the initiative.

"That's more like it!" Ruby encouraged her. "Go get that attractive American, whoever he is!"

"A green card wouldn't be too bad, I agree." Joe shrugged.

"Oh good God! What about an American who also has British citizenship?! Pure freedom!" exclaimed Ruby.

"Then you'd pay taxes in two countries!" Joe grimaced.

"I'm not going to do it for a citizenship or visas. Come on you guys, don't be like that! Stop digressing!" Tessa demanded.

"You want to do it to spite Brandon." Ruby said.

"No, that's not it." Tessa replied.

"My dear, repeat after me: 'I don't care about Brandon anymore! I don't need him!'"

"I don't care about Brandon anymore! I don't need him!" Tessa exclaimed, and Ruby proudly approved.

A deep voice came from the doorway. "I need someone to cover the phone lines. There are some calls on hold." Philip had arrived in all of his regal glory. The group's manager greatly resembled King Triton, father of Ariel. Minus the beard. And the trident. "I think break time is over."

"I think the only real break I'll ever get is gonna be in my coffin." Ruby muttered in astonishment, taking her coffee cup with her.

•

Minutes later, at her desk, Tessa slammed the table with both fists and only half-hearted restraint. She would've risen to her feet, but the wires on her headphones had other ideas.

"Of course, madam. As I just explained, you can bring your puppy to our property." She tried a fake smile, hoping it would calm her down.

"Great, I just want to let you know that my Lulu is allergic. Do you have carpets in the room?"

"We can remove the carpets, ma'am."

"Wonderful. One more question and then I'll leave you alone. Haha."

Tessa prepared her fist and felt the urge to strike her desk rising once more.

"Do you have parking spaces?"

"We do, yes."

"Is there parking in front of the building, or behind the building?"

"It is underground parking."

"Wonderful. I don't drive, you know, I come by tube."

Tessa turned her chair to Ruby, who raised her eyebrows. No words were necessary — Tessa's expressionless visage made it clear that her frustration was about to overflow once more. Ruby put two fingers to her temple and shot herself with an imaginary gun.

"But do you know by any chance, can you take the elevator from the underground parking lot?" the client continued, drawing Tessa's attention back to the conversation.

"Using the elevator, ma'am, yes." she replied.

"You know, my Lulu is allergic to exhaust fumes. I'm afraid the smell from the underground persists while in the elevator too. Haha. But you know what? I now realised that my Lulu won't join me in July. I do personally like carpets. What kind of carpets do you have in the room? You know, I saw some pictures online, and you have those rooms with green carpets, and I think green is depressing. Do you have anything more orange or red?"

The pens on Tessa's desk jumped as her fist hit the table once more.

●

Tessa sat down in front of her manager. King Triton's smile was friendly, if a little strained. Tessa kicked the carpet under her chair impatiently.

"I know you're overworked, and I understand," he said. "But look, don't take it personally. It's just phone calls. Try to relax."

She accidentally hit her toe on the table leg.

"I am relaxed."

"I understand. I just want to point out that we're always trying to keep the noise down in the office, which means that we externalise ourselves as little as possible."

He picked up two stress balls, leaving them on the table.

"Squeeze these balls next time."

●

At 6 pm, Ruby turned off the light in the office while Tessa waited by the door. They were both eager to get out of there.

"Any interesting plans this weekend?" Ruby asked, making sure she locked the gate behind her.

"No, nothing special. You?"

Ruby shook the gate, finally managing to lock it and enter the security code.

"I'm going to that cardboard show with Arif."

"Cardboard show?" Tessa frowned.

"Yes, you know… Barbican Centre. They put up some cardboard displays cut into various shapes. I think they're meant to represent special stages in our lives, depending on their size and texture. Or something like that anyway."

"So it's an exhibition then. Something like Tate Modern?"

"Exhibition! That's the right name for it!" Ruby laughed, a little embarrassed. "Can't wait!"

"You don't really care about that cardboard." said Tessa, looking at her colleague's gaze.

"Uhm. Not really."

"You're not interested at all."

"Mm-no. I think it's stupid." Ruby concluded.

"It's dull."

"Great nonsense."

"Right."

"I go for the drinks he buys me afterwards." Ruby laughed.

"There it is." Tessa shook her head and smiled.

"Anyway, it's Friday night. The night is long, and you, from now on, have to pay a lot more attention to yourself," she said, grabbing her friend's shoulders. "No crying, no regrets. Forget him, give him to the sharks. From now on, he's dead."

"That's what I'll do." Tessa smiled.

Later that night, Tessa's bed was lined with discarded chocolate wrappers. Slices of cold pizza in their box on her windowsill. Rain rolled down the windowpane as droplets fell from her cheeks to her bed.

"These are happy tears!" she shouted as if trying to justify herself. "Freedom tears."

February

March

April

May

June…

CHAPTER TWO

On Saturday morning, Maggie was pushing the stroller with her baby still sleeping inside. Her three-year-old daughter was running around the shopping centre.

Maggie had been an employee of the same call centre company for over four years now. But because she had spent almost two of them on maternity leave, she preferred to mention that she had belonged to the team for two years — two years and a bit.

"What do you mean he wanted to see other people?!" Maggie got angry, just catching up on the news.

"And this is where I had enough." Tessa concluded.

"Excuse me for saying this, but this guy's a prick."

The baby started crying. Maggie picked him up and tried to rock him back to sleep.

"I know, I know. But I got rid of him in January. Which kind of still scares me." Tessa spoke, gesturing.

Maggie noticed that her daughter was trying to pluck a potted plant and eat it, just a few steps away.

"Don't!" she exclaimed in a rush, running towards her, still holding the baby. "Don't put that into your mouth."

Maggie then returned, bringing the two children with her. The girl immediately found another distraction near the windows next to Tessa, playing with a mannequin.

"What scares you?" Maggie continued, taking her seat back on the bench.

"That I'm alone now–and I'm aging. Time flies!"

"It literally happened this year."

"That's not what I'm talking about. I wanted to start a family sometime. My clock is ticking and soon I'll be too old to conceive any kids at all!"

Maggie's daughter had meanwhile dug into her nose, wiping her palm off a store window.

"Don't pick your nose, baby!" Maggie shouted from a distance. "Not on that glass, please. You have a napkin in your pocket."

"It's a lost cause." Tessa sighed.

"My dear, you're twenty-three years old." Maggie muttered, and then the baby vomited on her shoulder.

Tessa handed her the handkerchief.

"I know. And you're twenty-nine and have two beautiful children. Whatever happens, you have them both. If I don't have the right person now, what will I do when I reach my 30s?"

Maggie cleaned her coat.

"I will close my eyes today, I will open them tomorrow and I'm thirty years old. I will close them tomorrow, I will wake up the day after tomorrow and I'm forty. When the chances of having children are gradually decreasing. I will close my eyes the day after tomorrow and will wake up the day after the day after tomorrow, when I'm fifty. Then I blink once more and I'm sixty. Then I'm dead."

"Okay. I don't think that's how it works. You can keep blinking in peace. That won't make you wake up from decade to decade. And you won't die at sixty."

"Who dies at sixty?" Rebecca then asked, joining the group, bringing coffee with her.

Rebecca was the kind of colleague who was eternally tired, constantly bored, always sarcastic, and relentlessly ready to express her aversion towards London. According to her own words, the city was intense, crowded, and stank of marijuana. She was reminded every day of how much she regretted leaving Milan.

"What's with thc silcncc?" she repeated. "So who dies at sixty?"

"Tessa. Apparently," said Maggie, swinging the baby who had just fallen asleep. "She was thinking of getting married. Now all her plans have been shattered."

"I didn't say that."

"Getting married?! Are you insane?!" Rebecca exclaimed.

“Shh!” Maggie warned Rebecca, as she placed the baby back inside the stroller.

“Sorry.” she lowered her voice. “Are you crazy, Tessa?!” she continued, whispering.

“Babies are cute." Tessa sighed.

“Okay. You're out of your mind. The only reason I’d put myself through having a crying creature pushed out of my body would be to disappear from that stinking office for at least a year.” Rebecca continued, glancing at Maggie. “Well done, sister!” Looking back at Tessa, “But anything else sounds crazy to me. Marriage? I've been with my guy for ten years. A decade! We're basically married. The only difference is, we're not. And here's the blessing. Believe me, you don't want a ring on that finger. Keep it naked.”

In the background, Maggie’s daughter took a pair of trousers off a mannequin. Maggie got up and ran towards her.

“Leave those clothes where they are!”

•

Monday. 9:30 am

Tessa pushed her chair towards Ruby, hiding her phone under the desk like a high school student. Philip rose slightly from his chair, only to sit down again, coughing briefly but significantly from behind his desk on the opposite side of the room. Ruby rolled her eyes and Tessa sighed, gently pushing her chair back to her desk. Tessa started up Skype.

"You can't even breathe in this office." Tessa typed.

“Tell me about it.” Ruby replied, stringing a whole row of emojis as usual.

“I'm installing one of these dating apps. But I don't know which one’s better.”

"Are you sure you want to walk down this dark path?"

"What could be darker than being sad and alone?"

“I don't know, Tessa, I'm too old for these apps. Good luck.”

Tessa turned slightly from her chair just to look Ruby in the eye, who in turn, faced her to do the same. Ruby shrugged.

“After all, you have nothing to lose. Have fun.” Ruby spoke.

“Ruby, the plan is to get married by next year. December is the deadline.”

“Deadline for what?”

“To be proposed to.”

"It's going to your head. It's June.”

"It's gone to my head for a while now already.”

A few raindrops hit the office window.

“Okay. Then, I’d say… at least pick an app that's rumoured to be more or less serious.”

Philip's cough was heard again from behind his screen. Ruby let out all the air she had held in her lungs, returning to her work for which she wasn’t paid enough to care about anyway.

●

Ruby unlocked her apartment door, turned on the light in the hallway, and took off her shoes, tossing them next to a closet. She walked barefoot to the living room, where she threw her purse on the couch. She turned the living room lights on, only to be panic-stricken by Arif, who was sitting next to her TV holding a glass of liqueur in his left hand.

“You scared me!” she laughed, touching her chest with one hand.

Ruby headed for the kitchen, where she poured water into a glass. There were a few bottles of alcohol on the table, which she noticed out of the corner of her eye but ignored for the moment.

"I didn't know you were in town this week." she returned to the living room, taking a sip of water and placing the glass on the table.

“I had a contract to sign so I came back earlier.” he muttered, staring blankly at the carpet under the table.

“Okay. Cool.” Ruby smiled, sitting down next to him.

“It's seven o'clock.”

“The night is long, we’ve still got enough time to have fun.” she replied, holding out a hand to caress his cheek.

Arif pushed her wrist away in one move.

"Just as you had fun before you got home!"

“What are you talking about? I went shopping.”

“And what did you buy?”

His now harsh tone froze the air.

“Nothing,” she replied. “I did some window shopping.”

Arif bent one of the beer cans in his fist and threw it on the floor. He got up and hurried to the bathroom, where he noisily turned the lock. Ruby looked around, at the mess inside the flat. She knew it was once again one of those days when anything she said could’ve been turned against her. Arif rushed back into the living room, his eyes clouded. Ruby stood up.

“Are you on anything at the moment?” she asked with a sigh, as he hurried closer.

His heavy palm threw her back on the couch.

"I'm not here for you to hold me accountable!" he exclaimed, pointing his finger at her.

Holding her jaw, Ruby didn’t dare to stand up, but frowned.

"Why are you here, then, Arif?"

He stretched his arm over her to lift his jacket. Ruby avoided eye contact.

"I don't know what's been going on with you lately," he muttered. “Because I don't like what I’m hearing lately and I hate what I see.”

Arif headed for the door, so then Ruby gathered her courage.

“What do you hear? What do you see?”

He looked at Ruby as he put his coat on.

“People are talking, Ruby.” he murmured, then slammed the door behind himself.

“About what? What are people talking about?” she whispered, then realised that she was all alone.

●

St. Paul's station, shortly before 8 am. A huge crowd. People were tactfully moving towards the exit. If you didn't know how to navigate your way out, you were likely to be trampled over before you’d even got to climb one stair.

"Metro! Good morning! Metro!" an employee's voice could be heard, sharing the morning newspaper, as he was standing in his same old perimeter right at the exit, in front of the railing that delimited the two lanes.

Tessa squeezed herself through the mass.

"Morning! Metro!" the employee repeated, smiling, as he expressed his friendliness towards every passer-by who didn't respond to his greeting. "Morning!" he added, cramming a newspaper into Tessa's hands, urging her to take it.

Almost ready to refuse, she looked into his eyes, feeling the need to do what she was told. Tessa took the newspaper and stepped aside. She leafed through the pages, until an ad in the corner of the page caught her eye. It was as if she knew she was looking for something, although she didn't know what it was. Without caring about anything else, she scanned through a dating app advert. A second later, she had downloaded it on the her phone. The screen light aggressively invaded her eyes.

"*June Storm*," she whispered, reading the front page title before proceeding to enter her personal details…

●

Tessa felt a light breeze on her cheeks.

"Wherever this app may take you, you promise not to question the Universe's magic" was the only clause that needed to be ticked.

"Okay..." she muttered, raising an eyebrow.

A pop-up window immediately opened, giving her a voucher for a drink of her choice. Tessa smiled, because the name of the pub was *June Storm*. The voucher was only valid after confirming at least one completed date on the app. The pub's address was in Chinatown. Tessa had now completely forgotten that she was in a hurry, like each morning. She had forgotten about everything else, because now she had discovered a new corner of the Internet…

●

Rebecca had just arrived at the office, dragging her feet on the carpet to her computer by the window.

"Morning!" Ruby greeted her as she retouched her lipstick, without looking up, because she was too busy with the mirror she was holding.

"I hate you all, don't talk to me until I have caffeine in my veins. Thanks." Rebecca muttered, but loud enough to be heard.

"Good morning, cheerful!" exclaimed Fiona, sticking her head out from behind the monitor, scratching her upper lip. "Can you help me with–"

"No." Rebecca muttered in response. She picked up one of the dirty cups she had on her desk to refill it with fresh coffee, already heading towards the kitchen.

The animosity between Rebecca and Fiona was unquestionable. Even though the latter struggled daily to integrate, Rebecca made sure to feed her a little — just a little bit of bitterness daily. Enough to make it clear that between the two, there would never be anything more than nought.

Tessa also arrived in a hurry, a little late, running to her monitor, pressing a few keys to wake the computer up, wiping the raindrops from her forehead.

"Is it raining?" Ruby asked, confused.

"Pouring." Fiona answered, seated next to the window.

"Pouring." Tessa confirmed, tossing her wet jacket on the hanger and leaving the open umbrella on the floor.

Philip stood up. They all looked at their own monitors.

"Don't open that umbrella inside the office, please, it brings bad luck."

"And where do you want me to leave it?" Tessa asked in a serious tone, not trying to sound sarcastic.

"Not in the office." Philip added, taking his seat again.

Rebecca returned with a cup full of black coffee.

"Come on, boss, stop being so superstitious."

"I'm not."

"Yes, you are."

"I'm not, I was just saying."

"You weren't just saying, you are." Rebecca insisted, until she reached her desk.

"I guess this one stays closed then." Tessa concluded, picking up her umbrella.

Philip rose to his feet again.

"Tessa, I can't see you in the system, can you log in, please? We got two incoming calls!" he started fussing.

"Aye-aye!" Tessa exclaimed, throwing the umbrella to the floor, which then opened on its own.

"But please, close that umbrella. I suspect misery is after us." Philip added, nevertheless.

Fiona tilted her head from behind the monitor, examining Rebecca for a few seconds.

"Can I ask you something now?"

"No." Rebecca replied short and dry, pulling her chair under the desk.

"I have a date today." Tessa spoke then, as she prepared some emails to be sent out.

"A date? What's that?" Rebecca commented, her disembodied voice hidden behind her screen.

"Ohhh! So those apps work!" Ruby excitedly turned her chair around to face Tessa.

"That's what I also just found out."

"Name?" Ruby asked.

"Giuliano."

"You're kidding?!" Rebecca snorted, getting to her feet to be seen. "Tell me he's not Italian!"

"He's Italian." Tessa confirmed.

"It's okay." Ruby spoke.

"There's nothing okay here." Rebecca fidgeted.

"That's because she's surrounded by too many Italians," said Fiona. "She was infected by you."

"You stay out of this," Rebecca spoke to Fiona, then turned her attention back to Tessa. "Listen, Italians are a bad idea."

"We're not." Ruby replied.

"Shut up, Ruby. We are."

"We're okay."

"We are, our men are not."

"Stop exaggerating." Ruby rolled her eyes.

"I'm not exaggerating, but how many Italians do you go out with?"

"None."

“See?”

"None because I have Arif."

“Oh, and Arif is very Italian!”

Tessa looked from one to the other, not feeling the need to intervene in the conversation.

“Instead, yours is Italian.” Ruby highlighted, pointing at Rebecca.

“Excuse me, mine was born in South America.”

"There's no difference here. He’s still Italian.”

“There's a big difference. It’s called mentality.”

“Mentality is mentality, that doesn’t change his blood.”

“It matters how he thinks, how he behaves…”

“Exactly. What am I trying to say here?”

"I don't know what you're trying to say, but you're wrong."

"Aren't you both trying to actually say the same thing?" Fiona interfered, sticking her forehead out from behind the monitor.

“You stay out of it.” Rebecca cut her short.

"Oh, yes, I'm sorry I was born British." Fiona muttered.

“I forgive you.” Rebecca replied, only slightly giving her attention.

“Leave her alone, let her see the Italian. Why are you so dramatic?!” Ruby exclaimed, raising both hands.

“I'm dramatic because that's how we are! Dramatic!” she shouted back, mimicking her gesture. “Drama! We live for drama! But we don't want men to be dramatic too. We are responsible for that drama. Not them!”

“Stop dramatising!” Ruby sighed.

“But that's the idea!”

"It's not. The point is, Tessa wants to go on that date today and she has every right to do so."

"But I didn't say she doesn’t have the right!"

“You didn't say it, but you're scaring her with this nonsense.”

"Scaring is a bit of a bold statement.” Tessa murmured. “But you're close.”

“Honey, go see your date today because you got all the rights to do so.” Ruby concluded, and her phone started ringing.

Ruby turned her chair back to her desk.

“Don't go!” Rebecca whispered to Tessa before she sat back in her chair.

“I hear you.” Ruby muttered, before answering the call.

Tessa took a deep breath, looking at her watch. Not even an hour had passed since she was at work. Philip stood up shortly, just to make sure his employees were spending at least a bit of their time working. Then he checked his system again, as a few calls seemed to be blocked somewhere on the line.

•

Piccadilly Circus was almost always crowded. Tourists, street performers and shoppers alike. The cocktail terrace, however, was slightly hidden away from the bustle. Giuliano arranged his sunglasses on his head and sipped on his cocktail’s paper straw, which started slowly fading away in his mouth.

"I hope you're having fun, my dear."

Tessa smiled and before she could say a word, he grabbed her fingers and kissed the back of her hand.

"You don't have to say anything. It is my honour to sit in front of this beautiful German woman, combined with… where did you say, was your mother’s side of the family from?”

"Well, my great-grandfather was Jewish. The fact that Hitler didn't kill him back then is why I'm sitting here in front of you now.”

“Oh.” he discovered, releasing her hand.

Tessa decided to gnaw on her straw, wondering if she had shared too much detailed information, too soon.

“Tell me, my dear, do you like pasta?”

“I like pasta.”

“Any preferences?”

“Not necessarily.”

“What do you usually cook?”

“Macaroni and cheese…?”

“Oh, very Americanised.”

“Pasta and chicken breast.”

Giuliano's left nostril flinched, as it was obvious on his face that something was bothering him terribly.

“Chicken… what?”

“Breast.” Tessa replied, sipping from her cocktail.

“My heart!” he sighed, grabbing his chest and getting to his feet. “Grandma would turn in her grave right now. The Americans have possessed your mind.”

Tessa was still sipping her cocktail.

“I am sorry,” he said, visibly saddened. “We shouldn't see each other again.” He left a banknote on the table to cover the drinks and putting his sunglasses back on his nose. “It is like my mother said: don't date outside your race!”

•

Ruby placed the cup of tea on the kitchen table.

“And he just left like that?!”

“Just like that.” Tessa confirmed.

“What an idiot.”

"He seemed genuinely offended."

“If he feels offended by that, he doesn't deserve your attention.”

“From what?” Rebecca mingled into the conversation, walking into the kitchen with an empty cup of coffee.

“Chicken breast.” Tessa said.

“What chicken breast?” Rebecca asked.

"I told him I sometimes cook chicken breast with pasta."

“Wait. Let me understand.” Rebecca took a deep breath. “You mean, like, you’re boiling chicken and adding that to the pasta?”

“Yes.” Tessa shrugged.

“My soul and my remaining days on this planet...!” Rebecca exclaimed, holding her heart, making an extravagant turn and leaving the kitchen.

“He at least paid, didn’t he?” Ruby tried to confirm.

“He paid, yes.”

"Italians... But one thing is for sure, they always pay.”

Tessa and Ruby raised their cups in sync.

"Did I tell you he mentioned his mother?" Tessa added on the way to the hallway.

"No, you didn't," Ruby replied. "But I think I've heard enough."

●

Tessa was standing in front of *June Storm*. The pub was on the exit road to *Chinatown*. She was looking at the picture of an attractive model on her screen. Lowering her phone, she stepped into the pub and looked around. The only source of light was candles burning at every table as well as along the bar. Almost at once, some of the tension in her shoulders faded away. Tessa felt bizarrely comfortable here as if something held her captive like a magnet.

Vincent was sitting on a couch in the corner of the pub, and as soon as he found Tessa with his gaze, he raised a hand.

"Beautiful! Here!"

Seeing his face, which in no way corresponded to the pictures, Tessa tried not to make the theatrical grimace on her face too visible. He raised an eyebrow in a pretty odious manner, probably thinking he was a big hit. The moment he got up to greet her, Tessa made a quick turn on her heel, looking for the way out without thinking too much. Vincent hurried to grab her wrist. Tessa realised she had no escape. At the same time, she reconsidered this situation, as she didn't want to seem rude either. Trying to forcibly smile, Tessa faced him benevolently. But seeing his smug grin, she was once again sorry that she didn't choose to just leave when her opportunity arose.

"And what preoccupied you today, before making your way to meet Vince Charming?" he asked, pointing at the space next to him on the couch.

"Methods of suicide." she murmured, sitting down, already analysing the menu.

"Don't worry, beautiful, Vince Charming won't kill you, he'll just take your *breathe* away."

"You mean, *breath*?"

"Yes, love."

"I think you'll give me asthma."

The bartender approached them politely. His nonconformist sleeves were rolled up all the way to his elbows and his hair was combed to the left, somehow vintage. His smile emanated mystery, as did the rest of this place.

“My name is Colin and I’ll be serving you tonight. What can I bring you to begin with?”

“Red wine please,” Tessa said to him, almost in despair. “Two glasses, actually.” She then took out her phone. “I’ve got a voucher.”

Colin smiled and gallantly bowed his forehead.

“Another gin for me.” Vincent ordered.

Colin looked from Tessa to Vincent, who stretched his arm behind her on the couch.

“Of course,” he smiled.

A few blocks away, Ruby was walking with Arif, but as she was already slightly tipsy, she held onto his arm to keep her balance on her high heels. Passing through the noisy pubs of Soho and bypassing the people sitting outside for a drink, the two turned towards a less busy street. The echo of Ruby's heels could be heard in a repetitive rhythm, for every two steps she was dragging one foot after herself, struggling to keep up.

“You're making a fool of yourself.” Arif spoke, trying to make her stand up straight, holding her elbow.

“Sorry.” she laughed.

“You drink too much.” he added, in a serious tone.

"You drank more than I did!"

“Yes, but I can handle my alcohol.”

“You know I’m not a good drinker.” she laughed. “You should’ve stopped me!”

“Maybe you’re right,” he exclaimed suddenly, pushing Ruby against the wall. “Maybe you need someone to give you a few more restrictions.”

Ruby shook her head to recover from the jolt.

"Maybe I’m tipsy, but you're crazy!" she shouted then, as Arif picked up the keys she held in her pocket and slapped her across the cheek with them.

Back at *June Storm*, Tessa was sipping her second glass of red wine. Colin was watching them from behind the bar as he was wiping his glasses.

“And how many sexy Danish guys have you dated before?” Vincent asked, raising an eyebrow again, still leaning on the couch arm.

"Well, I should say you're the first.” Tessa replied, avoiding eye contact.

"And your ex was English?"

“No.”

“What was he then?”

“BBC.” she replied, taking a larger sip of wine this time.

“BBC?” he asked, genuinely confused. “He was the British Broadcasting Corporation?”

“British Born Chinese.”

“Oh, my God! I’m sorry. Did he also force you to eat roasted cats and dogs with him?”

Tessa swallowed the rest of the wine.

"Excuse me for a moment, please." she said then, picking up her purse and getting up from the table.

She rushed downstairs to the loo, where she collided with bartender Colin, who seemed to be, somehow, ubiquitous.

“Sorry.”

“You okay?” he asked.

Before giving a generic answer, Tessa looked around. There was no one.

"Can I ask you a favour?"

“Date gone wrong?” he laughed.

“He’s not what he pretends to be.”

“What do you mean?”

“I don’t want to be rude, but he’s ugly in person. I still would’ve enjoyed a conversation, if he wasn’t so full of himself.”

“Can I see?”

Tessa pulled out her phone, leaving it in his hands. The bartender ruffled through a few pictures.

“Oh!” Colin then exclaimed. “Oh!” he grimaced, almost in pain. “Yes, I understand what you're saying. You're right, my dear,” he added. “You know what, I can’t see any more of this.”

Colin browsed through Tessa’s dating app and reported Vincent's account. With a big, satisfied smile on his face, he typed “Sorry, not sorry” as a reason for his decision and handed Tessa her phone back.

"That's better. I can't see you suffer any longer, my dear." he sighed, with a high dose of feminine compassion inside his chest.

Leading her to the back exit, he opened the door for her:

"Run, my dear!" he insisted, almost begging Tessa to hurry up.

Tessa smiled with gratitude; and stepping on the doorframe, she turned only once more to face him.

"Are you single?" she asked out of curiosity.

"I'm gay, my dear." he said, smiling lovingly at her.

"Ah, what the hell! But as they say, all good men are gay, or married."

As Ruby walked home alone, Tessa found her way to Leicester Square station.

A notification made Tessa stop right at the top of the stairs.

"Hey! Are you out tonight? Maybe we can see each other for a drink." was a message sent by Michael, another new acquaintance of Tessa's.

"Well, why not." she spoke to herself, shrugging, typing back.

Arriving at home, Ruby threw her purse on the floor and locked herself inside the bathroom, where she looked at herself in the mirror as the tap water was flowing. She washed her face. The blood got cleaned away, but her wound remained across her cheek.

Tessa hugged Michael, who arrived at the same station not long after his last message.

"I booked a meal at a nice place." he said.

"Great, which way are we going?"

"This way." he pointed.

Minutes later, Tessa realised she was standing again in front of the same *June Storm*.

"Oh no." she whispered, and then Michael forced her to step forward.

"I've got a voucher from them," he said.

Crossing the threshold, Tessa made eye contact with Colin, who was just as surprised to see her again, as was Vincent, who raised a hand when he saw her:

"My beautiful!" Vincent exclaimed, excited to see Tessa again.

"Ah, shit…!" she murmured, scratching her forehead.

"We have a reservation." Michael spoke to Colin, who approved after a brief hesitation of skepticism.

He led the two to a table towards the end of the pub. As soon as

Tessa and Michael sat down, Vincent approached them filled with enthusiasm. Stopping right next to Tessa's chair, he took a deep breath so that it didn't look like he was panting after just a few steps. He adjusted his fringe behind his ears, only to wrinkle his ridiculous forehead again.

"Honey, I was worried. Is everything okay?"

Tessa sighed.

"Who's this?" Michael asked.

"Sorry, I don't know who he is." Tessa said, hoping she could become one with the chair she was sitting on and disappear.

"But we just started to know each other!" Vincent insisted.

"Please leave, it was a bad idea."

"Do you know him?" Michael asked.

"Yes, I lied. I know him. I mean, it's not like I actually do know him; but I kinda know him." Tessa replied. "But he lied first!" she added, pointing at Vincent.

"But my beautiful, I would never lie to you!" he exclaimed.

"I'm not *your* beautiful!" she clarified. "And please don't —"

Vincent sat down on the chair next to Tessa, not letting her finish her sentence.

"Okay." she sighed. "Okay. It wasn't nice of me. But you lied first."

"She asked you to leave her alone." Michael interfered.

"Well then." Vincent went through a sudden change of attitude. "If that's what you want. I won't waste any more of my precious time on you."

"Please." Tessa sighed.

Vincent theatrically pushed his chair back, slamming some cash on the bar counter on the way out, making himself invisible. Colin watched him, then made eye contact with Tessa. She took a deep breath.

"What an idiot!" Michael muttered.

"Sorry."

"No, it's not your fault."

Colin appeared, bringing a few drinks on a tray.

"Enjoy your evening."

"What's left of it." Tessa laughed.

The clock on the wall showed that time had passed by fast. The pub was right before closing. The last customers were heading out.

“And I always say that too, chivalry has completely disappeared from the face of earth! No one today knows how to hold a door open or drive a woman home. You know, little things. It's very sad.”

“Don't be discouraged. Us nice guys still exist.”

“Yeah, but you know,” Tessa spoke, emptying her glass of whiskey. “After all, bad guys are still gonna win us over. Because we friendzone nice guys. That's how we operate and we can't help it. Mankind needs more people like you. Don't change, please.”

“Well!” Michael shouted suddenly, putting all the empty glasses aside with one hand. “Damn all women who think like that! I won’t change!” he added, more than just tipsy, wiping his lips with the back of his hand. “Damn you too! I will continue to be a good guy!”

Not long after, Colin unlocked the back door for Tessa, so that she could elegantly and subtly, once again, make her way out.

“You're sweet.”

"Take care, get home safe!" he patted her on the shoulder.

●

Tessa walked across the front yard of her house, trying to light the way using her phone since the streetlight had left her and the neighbours high and dry again.

Talking about neighbours, her middle-aged landlady appeared with rushed steps like a ghostly figure, wearing only a bathrobe. Gesturing wildly, she stood in front of Tessa, who turned her phone screen off and on again, only to continue to see her neighbour's insistent gaze.

“I have to ask you to stop leaving my fence open. Foxes walk into my yard at night and urinate on my lawn.”

"I never left your door open. I use my entrance, which doesn't involve crossing your lawn.”

“I didn't say you were crossing my lawn. I said you left my door open.”

“Neither.” said Tessa, trying to get around the annoying lady, but failing.

"But foxes urinate on my lawn! You know that grass is freshly planted up there. Four nights in a row, every morning at 3 am, I have to get out to chase foxes!"

"I hope you get more sleep from today on." Tessa concluded, bypassing her and walking towards the entrance of her home.

In the hallway, she tossed her trainers to the wall and headed for the kitchen.

"Bro! Behind you! Behind you! He's coming!" Imo, her housemate, was heard shouting from the living room as he was playing on his Xbox. Tessa had never understood the exact purpose of these games. "Nooo! He killed me. I'm dead, bro. That's it. he added, leaning his back against the couch in disappointment.

Imo was the kind of housemate who spent most of his spare time at home. Not because he had no friends, but because all of his friends were, in turn, obsessed with video games. Games, they apparently could only play from home. From their own houses, but in a team; communicating with each other through headphones.

"Farisita attacked me again." Tessa shouted from the kitchen so she could be heard.

"What did she want?" Imo shouted back from the living room, starting a new game.

"To tell us to stop leaving the door to her garden open. I don't even go there. She says foxes are pissing on her lawn. She's bored at home again and has no soul to bother."

"Ha!" Imo laughed, without looking up from the TV screen. "She's an idiot, in my opinion. I'm the one who's leaving the door open."

Tessa left her lunchbox she was preoccupied with back on the table and hurried to the living room.

"Why would you do that?"

"In my opinion, there's nothing cooler. You gotta see her running after that fox with a broom in her hand, at 3am! The best thing ever, *Imo*." he laughed, trying at the same time to keep up with his game.

Imo, had received his nickname after his verbal tic. "In my opinion", "in my opinion", "in my opinion"... "Imo", was all he knew to say sometimes. However, he was a cool guy.

"I left some popcorn on the table by the microwave." he added.

•

“How… ugly?” Rebecca asked, tilting her head from behind the computer screen.

“I mean… he wasn’t the most charming out there, is all I’d say!” Tessa whispered.

Ruby was putting on makeup, occasionally looking towards the manager's direction, making sure he didn't see how she was wasting time.

"The problem is, he’s arrogant. I guess he thinks that he looks like those photos for real. He probably thinks he's walking around with photoshop on his face. I could’ve gotten over it if he wasn’t so full of himself.”

"Nah, I don't think you want to close an eye when it comes to looks!" Rebecca grimaced “You should never do that! These kinds of people get even uglier as they grow older. Believe me, you don't want that.”

“We're all gonna be ugly when we're old." Tessa replied.

“Yes.” Rebecca agreed, before minding her work. “But not like the ugly ones.”

“And then?” Ruby asked, putting the powder back into her purse.

“Then I managed to escape, helped by that attractive bartender.” Tessa continued.

“Attractive? And single?!”

“Gay.”

“Ah, shit.”

"But Michael, who happened to be around by chance, contacted me."

“By chance, huh?” Ruby chuckled.

“Of course, always by chance,” Rebecca commented wryly. “Who’s Michael?”

"But he was weird, he started shouting.”

"Ah, damn this one too then!" Ruby sighed.

“Exactly.” Tessa approved.

Philip rose from his chair. They all turned back to their own desks. Tessa's phone started ringing.

“Here we go again…!” she muttered, rolling her eyes.

During the lunch break, Tessa collided with Joe in the kitchen, who was heating up his tomato soup in the microwave.

“Yo! How's it going?”

“I’m OK. Not really OK actually…” Tessa muttered, opening the fridge and rummaging for her lunch box.

“How’s your ex?” he asked, chopping some bread to toss into the soup.

“I don’t know. And I don't even want to know.” Tessa replied, walking to the microwave with her lunch box. “Are you done here?”

“Ah, yeah,” he said, taking his bowl. “I'm not hungry today, but I was thinking of washing my intestines with some soup. It's fresh, not canned. It's out of this bag.”

“And what makes you think soup out of a bag is fresh?”

Joe shrugged.

"When you're forty and divorced, and that didn’t kill you, nothing else will."

Tessa sat down at the table opposite Joe, who was standing while sipping his soup.

“And if you stay away from women, you can eat any kind of crap because you’re healthy and spiritually clean,” he said, making a large gesture with both hands. “The light inside is the most important!”

"I think my inner light will burn out completely if I keep digging inside that landfill any longer.”

"Why are you digging in a landfill?" Joe asked, confused, scratching his eyebrow.

“Because my time is limited.”

“You got cancer, what happened?” he asked while chewing on his bread soaked in tomato soup.

“I'm getting old!”

“I’m still not getting it here.”

“I think I'm having a mid-life crisis right now.”

"But you're not even twenty-five!"

“It doesn’t matter. Crisis is crisis! Better early than too late.”

"I don't think that's true in this case."

"I need to find a husband and have at least two children before I'm forty."

“I’m forty-four and I’m well and happy without children.”

"It's different for you men. A biological clock is following me. Do you understand?”

“Morbid.” he said, throwing the rest of his tomato soup down his throat like some sort of hot, savoury shot. “So what’s the remedy in this case?”

“Landfill.”

"What kind of rubbish are we talking about?"

“Men on dating apps.”

“Ah! Now we’re on the same page! What's the matter?”

“Scumbags.”

"At least I hope they do wash once a day!" he said, followed by a short moment of contemplative silence from both sides.

The two started laughing at the same time.

"Listen, the more guys you meet, the easier it will be for you. You know, in time.”

“In time? How much time?!”

“That depends now on what's on the market. I don't know what’s out there these days! I mean, these generations born after the '90s, I feel sorry for you… These kids have no manners, I don't know what's on their minds.”

“The '90s generation is okay. Those born after 2000 are the problem.”

“Are children born in 2000 adults?!” he exclaimed, taking a step back.

“Somehow, yes.” Tessa replied.

"I think I'm going to have my midlife crisis right now." Joe murmured, taking a seat.

●

"I'm really glad to meet you! Have you ever tried Malaysian food?” Oscar asked, with an insistently embarrassing smile.

“Yes. I had some chicken not long ago…”

“Next time, try our traditional food. It is made with coconut rice, anchovies and sambal sauce, served over a banana leaf. I can take you to a restaurant next time. Which Asian country would you like to visit first?"

"Thailand is on the list." Tessa said, her eyes scanning the rest of the room.

"Oh, I definitely recommend Thailand. People are so friendly and nice. Lots of wonderful beaches, exotic food and divine massages for only one hundred baht. Beautiful architecture. Many majestic temples. But my favourite country is Japan!"

An Englishman who was seated at the next table ordered another drink.

"I've never eaten a cat, but I've eaten dog." Oscar said suddenly, chewing on a french fry.

"Shh!" Tessa insisted, leaning forward and almost wanting to cover his mouth with both hands.

The Englishman choked on a sausage. Tessa then folded her hands in front and leaned back in her chair.

"And what did it taste like after all?"

"Duck." Oscar concluded.

The Englishman frowned and stood up to look for another table.

●

"That was quick! You arrived earlier than expected!" Tessa said to Jack, with whom she had just planned a date not long ago.

"I walk fast. I got long legs." Jack said. "Want to know what else is long?"

Tessa left *June Storm* and stopped in front of the stairs, watching a torrential rain unfold. Something was bringing her again and again back to this place. This time, for the first time in front of a thunderstorm. It rained quite often in London. But storms were pretty rare. Angry, she kicked the wall, immediately realising it was a bad idea. Dating. And kicking a random wall. Both together. Bad ideas. Searching through her purse, she pulled out her umbrella, struggling to open it.

Hastily, Tessa stepped into the street and opened the umbrella, which instantly turned upside down. In the middle of the wind, she struggled to put the umbrella back in shape. A sharp laugh mocked her. It sounded a lot like Amadeus — the movie character; because the real deal, may he rest in peace, might have had a different vocal cord. Tessa turned back up the steps and looked behind her to spot a well-dressed young man. Not too tall, but imposing enough, sucking on an electronic cigarette. His curly black hair was like a lion's mane covering half of his face. His shirt was slightly open, and his sunglasses hung from the first button. He laughed again, and his shrill voice got Tessa's attention.

"*June Storm* caught you without an umbrella." he amused himself.

Tessa looked at the broken umbrella she held in her hand. He drew another puff from his e-cigarette and blew raspberry-smelling steam into her face.

"Tell me about it." she muttered.

He detached himself from the wall next to which he was clinging, raising an umbrella.

"My name is Nev. Neville."

"Nice to meet you, Nev." Tessa said, then looked back at the street, where cars were passing by and the rain wouldn't stop.

"On the way back from the synagogue, I said to myself, today's gonna rain. And here's the rain!" he spoke.

"You're Jewish?" Tessa asked, looking back at him.

"Yes, does that bother you?" he replied, guzzling from his cigarette once more, letting out smoke like a passing train.

"No." she said. "My great-grandfather was a Jew."

"Ah, what a joy," he commented, then demonstratively raised his umbrella. "Are you going to the tube station?"

Tessa nodded. Nev stepped forward, raising his arm for her to join him.

"Let me lead you, milady."

"I'm good."

"We're going in the same direction," he said, taking another smoke. "But maybe you like walking in the rain." he added, pointing at the street. "I won't contradict you, nor do I have the right to stop you. My apology." he added, when he noticed that the cigarette smoke he was just exhaling was bothering her.

Tessa looked into his playful eyes, which were waiting for an answer.

"Okay." she agreed, grabbing his arm.

Nev opened his umbrella and together they walked down the

street. The wind was throwing raindrops in all directions.

"And what does an elegant, young lady like yourself do at such an hour in a place like this?"

“I went on a date.” Tessa replied as they both walked under the same umbrella towards the tube station.

“Ohhh! A date she says! Successful?”

“Not even nearly!” puffed Tessa.

“Ehhh! Life’s long.” he added.

“If you say so. It may be so.”

Nev laughed high-pitched, trying to keep his umbrella straight, as the wind was blowing it away.

“That's what I say and that's what it is!” he added, then placed the umbrella in Tessa's hands. “What’s your occupation?” he asked, suddenly running ahead in the rain.

“I just have a normal job that pays my bills. What do you do?” she asked, trying to keep up with him.

“I want to be an actor.” he spoke, then jumped into the first puddle that stood in his way, laughing maniacally.

"And how has that gone for you so far?" Tessa asked, as he jumped into the next puddle, then climbed on a railing to walk on it.

The lights of the buildings in the background were reflected in the puddles. Nev did a pirouette and the raindrops jumped out of his curly hair. He laughed again, slightly delirious.

“Pretty okay.” he replied, hurrying back to hide under the umbrella.

“The next Gene Kelly?” she asked, smiling curiously.

He took out his cigarette again, starting to smoke.

“No, not me.” he sighed. “But I’ll find my own way. A smoke?” he asked then.

“Thanks, I don't smoke.”

Arriving at Leicester Square, Tessa stepped up the first flight of stairs, then turned to look at Nev.

"It gave me great pleasure, milady." he said, stopping there, holding his umbrella.

"Didn't you say you were taking the tube?"

“I changed my mind.” he said, laughing again like an Amadeus brought back to life.

“As you say.” Tessa shrugged. “Then thank you for walking me here."

"A smoke?" he insisted, holding his cigarette friendly but firmly in front of her eyes.

Tessa wanted to refuse, but instead, without explanation, she did exactly the opposite. Taking the cigarette from his fingers, she inhaled a smoke. Then gave it back to him right away.

"It'll make you feel as if you've just stepped into a parallel Universe. Anything you wish to have, is already in your possession. Everything else you need, is already on the way." he stated, bowing gallantly. "A beautiful evening, elegant young lady."

"Good night!" Tessa amused herself, turning to go downstairs.

After a few steps, Tessa turned to look back. There was no sign of Nev; and the rain didn't cease either.

CHAPTER THREE

Friday night. Sri Lankan restaurant

Fiona played with a glass of wine without actually drinking it because she couldn't tolerate alcohol. She didn't tolerate many culinary dishes either, though she was at least willing to try. At the same time, Rebecca was trying to pull her chair further away from Fiona. Because she considered it was enough for her to have to cohabitate with Fiona at the same desk for over eight hours a day, let alone lunch breaks. Maggie also arrived, this time childless. But as restless and sleepless as the rest of the days when she made eye contact with the outside world. Rebecca grimaced at the menu.

"They've only got snazzy drinks. I didn't expect this." she rolled her eyes.

Ruby briefly opened her purse and let Rebecca peek inside.

"I've got some beer with me."

Tessa was leafing through the menu as well while Philip inhaled and exhaled, visibly irritated.

"We should've gone to the Greek restaurant I mentioned."

"Stop being so racist!" Maggie pointed out, trying to lower the volume at which he just expressed himself.

"I'm not racist!" he retorted, attempting to keep his voice down. "But it's pretty expensive here."

"You're not gonna pay anyway." Rebecca snorted, lifting two glasses of Prosecco from a tray before the waiter could even do his job.

“It's not about who pays. But you know that the company has a specific budget, which we could’ve used, with a better plan, elsewhere. But now, we can't change anything anyway.”

The waiter walked away.

“Then relax!” Rebecca exclaimed, raising a glass in his honour.

Ruby leaned towards Tessa.

“Plans for this weekend?”

“Not really.” Tessa replied.

“Details.”

“What details?”

“Reasons, actually.” Ruby corrected her words.

“What reasons?” Tessa asked, still confused.

“No date, nothing?”

Tessa sighed slightly annoyed.

“I don't know, I think I'm taking a step back from the market. It's full of weirdos.”

“The world is full of weirdos!” Rebecca intervened. “We're all weird.”

"I don't know if I want to approve of what Rebe just said, but I'd say: don't give up so easily."

Suddenly, *Rigoletto: La Dona E Mobile* started playing in the background. Rebecca grimaced.

“Oh, great. This restaurant is very thematic, as if it felt that we were here. I was expecting some Indian music instead. But Italy is everywhere, where Italians are, apparently.”

“Racist!” Maggie added.

“That's that music from the pizza commercial!” said Rebecca, listening around.

"How ignorant of you." Fiona laughed.

"If she talks one more time without being asked, I'll make her swallow that wine, glass included.” Rebecca hissed through her teeth.

The waiter returned. They all hid their faces in the menu. There was no real need for the dinner to be as sophisticated as it was, but since the company was paying for the evening, everyone went along with it. Rebecca was pushing her salad from side to side and Philip was already half poisoned by the spicy peppers.

“This food is too spicy.” Tessa whispered through tears.

"Don't be a pussy!" Ruby persuaded her, struggling to swallow some spicy guacamole herself.

"This is exactly what I needed!" Maggie rejoiced, being the only one who could apparently tolerate the menu.

Fiona hit her forehead on the table and fell asleep there, unclear whether from drinking, food, or other allergies. Rebecca put a finger between the table and Fiona's nose to make sure she was still breathing.

"Is she alive?" Ruby asked.

"Unfortunately," said Rebecca, straightening her back. "I also just felt her moustache. Floundering like grass in the wind every time she exhaled."

"Ew." Ruby frowned.

"Ew." Maggie approved. "But that's rude, Rebecca."

"I need more wine to wash my nausea away." Rebecca spoke, motioning at the waiter and then at the empty glass on the table.

Dessert was served, inhaled, and vacuumed away by Philip with the greatest haste. He then excused himself, rising slowly and slightly embarrassed. This move quickly became a panicked run towards the loo. Fiona looked on, unperturbed.

"I have a weird feeling in my stomach," Rebecca muttered. "I think it's time to go home."

"Literally? Or you just have a hunch about something?" Ruby asked, confused.

"I have a hunch that something wants to escape from my gut!" she exclaimed, jumping out of her chair and running down the hall.

"Philip knew what he knew." Ruby shrugged.

"Are you referring to the fact that he ran to the loo, or that he recommended a Greek restaurant instead?" Tessa asked.

Ruby shrugged again.

"Philip knows what he's talking about." Fiona woke up, slowly raising her head from the table, still dizzy. "But you have to learn to listen to him."

Without hesitation, Ruby picked up Rebecca's still-full glass and grabbed Fiona by the chin.

"Come on, open your mouth." Ruby insisted, forcing Fiona to drink all the contents.

Fiona's head fell back on the table.

"So, where was I?" Ruby spoke.

"I think it's time to leave." Tessa replied.

“You go ahead. I ordered another portion.” said Maggie.

"Are you sure you're not pregnant again?" Ruby asked, just to clarify.

“Leave her alone, it’s paid by the company anyway.” Tessa spoke, rising to her feet.

“Are you gonna take care of that?” Ruby asked Maggie, pointing at Fiona.

“Do I have a choice?” Maggie sighed.

At the exit, Ruby checked her phone, then hugged Tessa.

"Go ahead, I'll meet Arif."

“Oh, spontaneous!”

“Spontaneous, why not?” Ruby smiled.

As Tessa turned to the next street, Arif appeared beside Ruby, taking her by surprise.

"Do you want a drink?" she asked, at which Arif frowned immediately.

“You already drank today!”

Ruby approached his chin and inhaled.

“You have as well.”

Without thinking, Arif grabbed Ruby by the shoulders, pulling her after him to the parking lot behind the building.

"I don't want anything to do with an alcoholic woman! I think I mentioned that before!” he said, then wrapped a hand around her neck.

Ruby looked into his serious eyes, not knowing if she could still recognise the person she once fell in love with. At last, deeply offended, she kicked his knee, and he backed away.

"And I don't want anything to do with you anymore!" she spoke, wondering for another moment if she had made the right decision.

Arif clung to her sleeve.

“Leave me alone!” Ruby exclaimed, then picked up her purse and hit him.

Feeling the satisfaction that had just invaded her chest, Ruby hit him again and Arif flinched.

“What the hell are you carrying in there?! Stones?” he shouted, shielding his head.

“Worse.” she smiled. “Beer.” she added, hitting him where it hurt the most.

•

At work, Tessa was washing her hands at the sink when Ruby, who had just come out of the toilet, joined her.

"Why have you never said anything?" Tessa asked. Her demand for an answer was more driven from mild outrage than curiosity.

"I didn't think there was anything interesting to mention." Ruby murmured, avoiding eye contact.

“No, it's not *interesting* in any way! It's violent. It's disgraceful!” Tessa pointed out, still holding her hands under the lukewarm water.

“It is what it is. It was what it was. I dumped him, he accepted it nicely and left. Everything is fine now.”

“Nothing’s fine now!” Tessa exclaimed, pulling on Ruby's collar, revealing the scratches on her neck.

“Hey!” Ruby reassured her, smiling and adjusting her coat. “I'm sorry I didn't tell you.”

Tessa turned the tap water off.

“No.” she spoke after a short pause. “I apologise for not realising what you're going through.”

“Okay.” Ruby laughed, somewhat awkwardly. “It's in the past, we leave it there and we never bring it up again.”

Tessa approved, but deep inside, something still worried her.

"But now tell me, when is your next date?"

Philip had not yet appeared to complain about the absence of two slaves from his garbage mine, so the two continued to enjoy their illegal break without any actual right to freedom. Taking her phone out, Tessa checked her messages.

“Today, after work.” she shrugged, relatively indifferent.

“Oh! Good job!” Ruby encouraged her. “Let the dates flow!”

“He sent me a three-minute-long voice message this morning.”

“Oh, talkative.” Ruby agreed.

“He was asking what I did yesterday. He said that on the way home on Wednesday, he saw a hostage in handcuffs, smoking with the cops.”

“Oh, he's also funny.” Ruby approved, almost sincerely impressed.

“I didn't answer immediately and then he sent another voice message after twenty minutes, informing me that if I was going to be just as chatty during the date, as I was during the morning, he wouldn't have room to talk because of me.”

“Aha, he got sarcasm on board as well! I already like him.”

“Ruby!” Tessa sighed.

“What?!”

“He’s starting to get annoying, and we haven't even met. When he first wrote to me after I left him my phone number, he said ‘Save this number to be appropriately enthusiastic about receiving my phone call.’”

"Interesting..." Ruby hesitated for a moment.

“A few minutes ago, he wrote about the hostage in handcuffs and the cops.”

“The one on Wednesday?”

“Nope, apparently it happened just now.”

“Okay, beware the attention seeker! Maybe he should keep track of the jokes he prepares in advance. What’s his job? Tell me he at least got money!”

“Finance, I think.”

“Perfect!” Ruby exclaimed, raising both hands.

“And he added that if I’m gonna be late tonight, he’s gonna deduct two points.”

“Two points from where?” Ruby asked, genuinely confused.

“See?!”

"I don't see any serious problem here! He’s just being funny!”

"Can I give you my opinion or should I abstain from it?" Tessa asked, narrowing her eyes.

“Listen, be excited for tonight, you never know where lightning could strike.”

“Okay, if you're positive, I am as well.”

“Tessa, I want to see you happy. You deserve it.”

“It's more complicated than that, don't you think?”

"That's why you have to go to as many dates as possible!" She held her fingers together in the Italian style. “Quantity.”

The two left the toilet, while Joe walked down the hall, holding a cup of water.

“Your boss is looking for you,” he spoke, blinking a few times in Tessa's direction. “You too.” glancing at Ruby.

“Okay.” the two approved in chorus, without moving.

"How long have you been inside there, you sneaky devils?” he asked, eyes narrowing with suspicion.

"You know that the deepest conversations always take place in the toilet." Ruby replied.

“Well yes, I suppose I can see that happening.” Joe conceded, as the two then headed for the office. “So that's why you always go in a herd.”

Ruby took a step back, turning to him for a second.

"Why do you drink water from a coffee cup?"

“Detox.” he replied.

●

Tessa arrived at the late-night bar she had never visited before. Inside, it was already sad and empty at 9 pm. Some tumbleweed was missing. Through the only halfway clean window, she noticed a silhouette that looked somewhat like a John, sipping from a cocktail. Tessa took a deep breath and gathered her courage. It wasn’t as if she needed to — at this point, the mere fact that she was present already demonstrated a decent bit of heroism in her book.

As she entered, John jumped out of the high chair he was sitting on. Tessa tried to smile and he greeted her with open arms. Not to hug her, but to wave them around for no reason. Just like a hen with great enthusiasm, followed by a few twists of his hips as he took a few steps back.

“You arrived a little early. Plus two points! Come on, sit down.” he pointed at a couch next to the table.

"I wonder if I shouldn't have made it at all." she muttered to herself, taking her jacket off and placing it on the chair.

“Did you say something?” he asked, grinning inappropriately.

“Yeah. I’m going to the ladies. Be right back.” she replied, smiling politely.

In front of the mirror, Tessa looked herself in the eye, trying to wonder why she was voluntarily forcing herself into such uncomfortable situations.

Returning to the table, she placed her envelope purse beside her and perched on a tall chair, as John sipped his cocktail.

"So what brings you here?" John broke the ice, nibbling on an olive he had from a previous drink. "Is your heart already pounding in your chest, thinking of me?"

Tessa stood speechless for a moment, then John snorted with laughter.

"Kidding. Kidding." he amused himself, waving his left hand. "You came here to try your luck with me."

Tessa looked at him, blankly.

"You don't want anything to drink?" he added.

"Now that you mention it, yeah. Be right back." she replied, forcing a smile.

Leaning both of her palms on the counter, Tessa smiled at the bartender, who represented a moment of escape for her. She felt that for at least a second, she was surrounded by a lucid human.

"What can I get you?" he asked, chewing noisily on some gum.

"Gin. Dry. Two." she spoke.

A blink later, the bartender placed the two glasses on the counter. Tessa brought her credit card closer to the reader, picked up the two glasses, smiled politely, and returned to her place. As she found her seat in the high chair and John was comfortable on the couch, the silence among the two started to be annoyingly penetrating. John was still gnawing on his olive, blinking at a brisk pace. Probably from a nervous tic.

"So, what are we starting with?" he asked.

"To start, what?"

"Tell me something about you."

"Oh." she agreed, taking a sip from her gin, and then another. "I work in a call centre. Nothing interesting. You?"

"I work in finance," he replied, chomping now in a bizarre way that might've been related to another nervous tic. "I got money." he laughed out loud, not unlike a dog barking at a brick wall. "Just the way girls like it."

"Haha." Tessa smiled briefly and forcedly, taking a larger sip of alcohol.

John then saw her purse and eagerly picked it up with both hands.

"Beautiful purse."

“Thanks.” she replied, holding out a hand to imply that she wanted it back.

“What’s it made of?” he asked, blinking uncontrollably.

“I don't know what it's made of, but it's designed to sit back there, where it was before you took it.”

“Looks like a *Pokémon.*” he added then, licking his lips, just as uncontrollably as before.

“A Pokémon?” Tessa tried to clarify, making sure she heard correctly.

“Yes.” he replied, then began to shake the purse. “What do you have in here? Make-up?”

Tessa stretched her arm across the table and retrieved her belongings.

“You think make-up is all women have in handbags?”

"Pretty much..." he shrugged. “But you look pretty low-maintenance.”

“Are you trying to say I’m not posh enough...?”

“Looks like you don't put much make-up on.”

“In conclusion, I’m not taking care of myself.”

“I didn't say that.” he blinked as he spoke. “But you'd be better off with longer lashes, I'd say.”

“Okay.” she agreed, emptying the first glass of gin and moving on to the second.

“Come on, come closer,” he said, fluttering his hand again. “Why are you sitting so far away from me?”

“I'm okay, thanks.” she smiled, feeling that familiar sense of rage welling up inside.

“You’re shy. I understand,” he concluded, licking his lips like a reptile. “You know what they say… it’s always the quiet ones.” he giggled, shaking his head slightly, trying to make her laugh too, but Tessa stayed absolutely still. “Let me ask you a few questions and you give me your answers.”

“Okay.” Tessa replied. Being almost halfway through her second glass of gin helped her transition into a relatively comfortable indifference.

“So. I'm testing you. Pay attention,” he said, raising his index finger, puckering his lips together. “It’ll tell me a lot about you.”

“Go ahead.”

"So, imagine you're driving on a road," he said.

“I don’t have a driving license.”

“Just imagine.”

“Okay, at your own risk.” she sipped her drink.

“You reach a strawberry plantation.”

“Okay.”

“You stop the car.”

“Okay.”

“And see the plantation.”

"I'm glad I'm not blind."

“You get out of the car because you feel like eating some strawberries.”

“Natural.”

"The plantation doesn’t belong to you."

“Obviously.”

"But you're thinking of tasting some strawberries."

“Naturally. I'm an immigrant, we're here to steal.”

“That's right.” He clasped his palms together while blinking repeatedly, which made Tessa rile up, forcing her to take another sip from her drink. “But the plantation is surrounded by a fence.”

The bartender listened in, munching on his chewing gum.

“How tall is the fence?” John asked then, proud of his exposition so far.

“Are you asking me? It's your story.”

“No, no! I'm testing you!”

“Ah, well I don't know…! Average height, I’d say.” she shrugged.

“Aha…! Interesting.” he nodded thoughtfully. “Typically female, I’d say. And yet it is not.”

Tessa seemed to be slowly losing her temper. And yet not.

“So. You’ve jumped over the fence.” he continued. “You see the strawberries.” He was licking his lips and blinking at the same time now.

“I see them. Fascinating.” she sighed, for she had emptied her second glass of gin.

“How many do you plan to pick?”

"A few..." she murmured, giving one more answer to satisfy his pleasure.

“I need an exact number.”

“Seven… eight?”

"Interesting..." he thought to himself. "Eight."

Tessa waited with raised eyebrows.

"That already tells me a lot about you."

The bartender got bored, so he threw his chewing gum into the bin and tried to find more busywork around the bar.

"I learned some important things about you today." John spoke.

"Astonish me."

"Come here, next to me, don't be shy." he said while taking her palm.

Tessa took her arm back.

"I'm fine here."

"As you wish. It's not like I'm forcing you." he stretched out an arm on the couch, involuntarily licking his lips.

Tessa looked at her watch.

"The fact that you chose to not make the fence too short, but not too high either, tells me that you encounter obstacles quite often in life."

"You've read that in some article that shouldn't exist for the good of mankind and you're now telling me about it."

"No, no! I studied it." he blinked in an intellectual but uncontrolled manner. "Strawberries are temptations. The fact that you stopped the car means that you can't help it."

"Can't help what? You told me to stop the car." Tessa frowned.

"Anything in general. Hmm. You're in denial. Interesting." he said, nonchalantly. "And the fact that you stole eight strawberries —"

"Imaginary. Strawberries." she interrupted him.

"The idea itself indicates that you can't keep your impulses under control."

Tessa blinked in confusion and John licked his lips again.

•

Returning to *June Storm*, Tessa lifelessly sat at the bar, her chin in her palm. Colin, who was wiping his glasses, helped her kill time.

"It's okay, my dear. You'll find your man and I'll find mine."

Tessa sighed.

"You know, you're the best thing that's happened to me lately."

"Come on, chin up," he said. "A horrible chap like me doesn't make your day better. There's more to see out there."

She laughed, patting him on the back of his hand.

"I'm serious."

In the background, someone pushed a chair around. Colin looked up.

"What a surprise! Who do we have here again?" said a voice.

Tessa didn't turn around. Nev stopped next to her, greeting Colin with a nod, then looked back at Tessa.

"You!" Tessa suddenly got excited.

He ran a hand through his curly hair.

"Nice to see you again, milady."

"I forgot your name." she exclaimed, pointing at him.

"Nev."

"Nev!" she smiled. "I'm Tessa."

Holding one hand behind his back, he grabbed Tessa's hand with the other, kissing the back of her palm.

"Busy tonight?"

"It was a disastrous evening."

"The evening is not over yet."

Tessa seemed sincerely amused.

"For me it is. I don't even know what I'm doing here. Or what I'm looking for."

"Me." Nev spoke. "Without sounding too weird in my statement. Something inside was telling me I should approach you. And before you say anything, no, I'm not trying to hit on you."

He propped his elbow on the counter. Tessa was waiting for the sequel of his narrative exposition.

"Do you want to go out for a drink?" he asked, pointing at the exit.

"I can't, it's late." she replied without hesitation.

"Come on, half an hour."

"Thanks. You're cute. But I have to refuse."

"It's my birthday..." he insisted.

Tessa thought for a moment.

"What are you doing? Are you not going to say 'Happy Birthday'?" Nev exclaimed.

"Happy Birthday!" she laughed.

"Come on, half an hour." he added, nodding his way out.

After another brief hesitation, Tessa got down from her chair.

"Fine." she agreed.

Colin withdrew with a smile.

The streets were still crowded. Nev looked around for a moment to orientate himself.

"You're a Gemini, then!" Tessa said.

"Yes." he acknowledged, then made a circle next to his own temple. "All Gemini are a bit of unsound mind."

"I understand."

"I don't think you understand, but I'm glad you're supportive." he replied, pulling out his e-cigarette, having a smoke.

"So where are we going?"

"Green Park?" he asked. "We can sit on the grass or on a bench, depending on what the lady prefers."

"Sounds good." she confirmed.

Then he approached her, opening his jacket in such a way that only she could see. He had hidden bottles of whiskey in his inside pockets. Nev looked jokingly from left to right, then whispered:

"I can provide these goodies, but if the lady has other preferences, we can satisfy them."

"Red wine."

"Let it be red wine, milady," he said. "The supermarket is in that direction." he pointed across the road. "Let's go!"

Passing by a remarkable number of dog-walkers, the two sat on the last rung of stairs opposite Buckingham Palace. Nev sucked from his e-cigarette, leaving behind a cloud of smoke.

"Sure not?" he asked, pointing to the plastic he held in his hand.

"Very sure." Tessa replied, making herself comfortable.

"It tastes like strawberries!" he insisted.

"Oh, please, I don't want to hear any more about strawberries!" she snapped.

"Okay, okay! I come in peace," he said, raising both his hands. "Therefore." he continued, taking out one of the whiskey bottles he had hidden in his jacket and opened the wine for Tessa. "Happy birthday to me!"

"Happy Birthday to you!" she exclaimed, and then he clinked his bottle against hers. "How old are you turning?"

"Irrelevant."

Tessa approved, holding the wine bottle in both hands and looking at the illuminated palace.

"So what's the matter with you? How's it going with the guys?"

Tessa looked up.

"How do you know?"

"How do I know what?" he asked, puffing. "Wait, don't be alarmed. I'm not a weirdo. The first time we met, you were leaving a date."

The muscles on Tessa's face relaxed and she immediately snorted with laughter.

"It's horrible, I have to admit. I know the world is full of weirdos, but I don't know how only I can attract each and every one of them. In a short period of time as well."

"Maybe because you're weird too," he said, sipping from his whiskey. "Like me. Haven't you thought about that probability?"

She thought for a moment, then took a sip of wine.

"No."

"But are you thinking about the future, milady?"

"Of course I'm thinking about the future!" she retorted.

"About the near future or the distant one? And how detailed?"

"What are you trying to say? Both, I think." Tessa watched Nev with a confused look on her face.

"What do you mean, you think? Do you only think or do you know?"

"I don't know. Give me an example."

"Tell me what you're most afraid of when you think of the distant future."

Tessa looked at the bottle of wine.

"To be exactly where I am now, at forty?"

"You mean here on these stairs, with me, alcohol and a brilliant view?"

"That's not what I mean!" she laughed.

"I know, I know." he sighed, taking one last puff, then putting the e-cigarette back in his pocket, just to take out another. "Does this bother you?" he asked, picking up a lighter.

"No." she shook her head.

"I'm most afraid of alopecia," he said after a moment of silence.

About to drown in wine, Tessa looked at him.

"My father is almost bald," he spoke. "He only has a few

strands of hair left. But to be honest, if alopecia jumps a generation, I'm the lucky one!"

"What are you trying to say?" she laughed in surprise. "You want your future son to be bald instead of you!?"

"I don't want that explicitly, but I wouldn't mind if the disease avoided me."

"I won't say no more. Maybe you should only have daughters. It's probably harder to pass on. However, you're bizarre."

"I know, I know." he sighed, lighting some weed, puffing around.

Tessa frowned, trying to purify the air with one hand.

"What cigarette is this?!"

"Ehhh. You don't want to know…!" he whispered, making himself comfortable and enjoying his vice. "But why are we talking about my non-existent baldness? Back to the more interesting topic: your non-existent partner."

"There's nothing interesting to discuss here."

"Don't worry! There is always something interesting! It's all about perspective." he said, raising his cigarette in the air and looking at it with only one eye.

She looked at him, waiting for him to continue with his statement or say another remark filled with philosophy. But instead, Nev burst into hysterical laughter. Tessa smiled too.

"You don't know what you want," he then said.

"What do I want?"

"You have to know."

"I know what I want. But life doesn't always give you what you want. It's the reality we live in."

"It's really one of the realities you live in." he agreed, sucking from his weed and slowly letting the smoke out of his chest. "But not the only one."

Tessa took a sip of wine and looked at the crosswalk, where the traffic light's colour changed.

"You alone attract these failed dates." Nev spoke, and his words caught her eye.

"What do you mean?"

"The losers you're complaining about. You attract them."

"Let me guess, because I'm a loser too!"

"No. Because you pity yourself, milady."

Tessa didn't answer. Then Nev jumped to his feet, raising both arms in the air:

"It's like waking up in the morning and saying: Dear Universe, give me even more of what I don't like!"

"Why would I do that?" she frowned.

"That's exactly what you do!"

Tessa avoided him for a moment, then looked at him again.

"I don't know what you're smoking there."

"You wanna try?" he asked, giggling, slightly more impulsive this time.

"No, thanks." she murmured.

"You're ignoring endless possibilities, refusing to change a single thought." he said, raising his finger almost like a conductor, and his curly hair fluttered in the wind.

"Which is...? Trying to smoke from your weed?"

"No!" he shook his head. "Forget about my weed, milady," he said, taking another puff of smoke. "Everything, absolutely everything, starts here!" he added, touching Tessa's temple with a finger. "The Universe's actions, reduced to a single thought."

And then, inexplicably, even though things hadn't started to make sense for Tessa yet, she felt that something had changed direction in the way she looked at the world surrounding her. Not as if she had found a new perspective — not by a long shot. But a new enthusiasm had come to life. A new hope that countless mysteries were waiting to be unraveled. Someday, somehow.

●

At home, Tessa threw her shoes down the hall and left her purse on the sofa in the living room. She then noticed Imo, who was sitting with both knees perched on the kitchen window sill, looking outside.

"What are you doing there?"

"Shh, T!" he whispered, then motioned for her to come closer.

Tessa walked next to him, trying to see what he was looking at. Imo sipped from his canned beer, looking enthusiastically at Farisita, who was desperately trying to drive a fox out of the front yard.

"You left the door open again." Tessa sighed.

"For your amusement too, housemate!" he said, opening another can. “Beer?”

“Why not…?” she shrugged, lifting her knees on the windowsill as well.

“How are the dates going?” he asked, his eyes fixed on the action taking place in front of the house.

”Terrible.” Tessa replied.

Farisita now lifted a baseball bat, throwing it at the fox. It stood there, in spite of it all, smiling like a Siamese cat. Tessa laughed.

“Ha! Told you it was worth the effort! I like to see her tormented at night.” Imo cheered, handing a bag of dry salami to Tessa. “Snack?”

“Sure,” she said, helping herself. “But don't you think that will make her even more deranged during the day?”

“Should we care?” Imo asked after a gulp of beer.

The two looked at each other for a moment, then looked outside at their landlady, who was desperately throwing twigs at the fox.

“Naaah!” the two concluded in synchronicity, clinking cans of beer.

CHAPTER FOUR

7 pm

Here she sat, on the last free seat on the Central Line. Peering out of the dark window, the last of the natural light disappeared as the tube went underground. It was always a bit too warm and a little disgusting, but the atmosphere always helped her relax. Her love for the Central Line couldn't be justified.

For most, it's a nightmare. But this one route was her favourite. The red line. Like a pounding heart. Straight and to the point. With well-defined stations that all made sense. No talking around the subject. Minimal fuss. Looking at you, Circle Line! Tessa had never been able to get used to the Circle Line either and she had no desire to even try. The Central Line gave her a sense of security. She knew she would reach her destination. The light wasn't too insistent, but not too diffused either. It was conducive to meditation.

Passengers crammed back and forth. Tessa smiled to herself as she had taken a seat at the right time. Another very important detail that contributed to her moment of silence.

These crucial moments in the morning always went by like this. Today, Tessa couldn't figure out the reason why she was confused. Sad and irascible as well. The source of this condition was certainly an external one. Definitely from the incomprehensible world of men. From that dark abyss, loaded with infantilism.

Tessa looked at all the pretty, smart-casual ladies, next to men wearing three-piece suits. They were all minding their own business, with their noses buried in either phones or newspapers. Maybe that was the problem; people are just so caught up in their own business that being self-centred becomes second nature. But what else could you be doing at seven o'clock in the morning on a dark train? Exactly. Sit back comfortably and enjoy your demons. That's what you could do.

"Time. That's what I need." she thought to herself. "Time solves everything."

But time itself was not exactly in her favour as a woman, as she already knew. Contradictions, contradictions, contradictions. There seemed to be no escape. We are born, we exist, we exist some more, we are disturbed by a job we hate and men with commitment issues, we exist a little more, and then we die. If we're unlucky, we might die prematurely due to something like liver cirrhosis. Maybe Tessa should cut back on the wine.

Life has to be lived somehow. With the good and with the bad. With or without men. Maybe that was the answer. Their absence equalled happiness. Undoubtedly, the final equation had been discovered. Who needed them? How hard could it be for them to be ignored?

The train reached St. Paul's Station and Tessa stood up to make her way to the doors. Citizens were preparing for attack. A sharp elbow helped Tessa lose her balance. At the same time, the hand of the same arm gripped her sleeve to restore her stability. Tessa immediately raised her head, looking straight into the eyes of a charming young man. Irrelevant in this story, but charming. Before she was able to analyse him too much, he alighted, disappearing into the crowd. And here, ladies and gentlemen, was another two-second romance. Which could have someday, somehow, become something much more significant. But the opportunity flew away. And going back to the previous statement: it was all a contradiction, a contradiction, a contradiction…

●

At the grocery store next to the office, Ruby tossed her armful of instant pasta and juice onto the checkout and rummaged inside her pocket for some change. Tessa handed her a voucher.

"What is this?"

"I got it from buying some chocolate. Take it. It's 50% off."

"Ohhh, we're livin' large! Thanks."

Tessa looked at her watch, tapping her leg.

"We have five minutes left. We should have been logged in already."

"Caaalm down. Calm down." Ruby assured her, shaking her head placidly. "You know statistics say that if you die from overworking yourself, your company would find to replace you within a week. Please value your life."

"It's nice that you're concerned about statistics like these before our shift, but I still think we'd better hurry up."

Ruby tossed the pasta into her purse next to the beer can she was saving for later and followed Tessa, who hurried out onto the street. A notification made her stop just before the traffic lights. Ruby took a step back. Piles of hurried citizens were crossing in both directions.

"What are we doing here? Are we stopped at a red light again? The only place where this still happens is Germany. And this is not Germany, my dear."

"I have a new match." Tessa concluded, still keeping her eyes on her phone.

"Nothing new either. They come in dozens a day. But as I know you well already… 'Quality, not quantity,' I don't bother to explain any more."

"He also just wrote. He seems friendly."

Ruby grabbed Tessa's elbow and pulled her over the crossing.

"First of all, you're not looking for friends right now. Secondly, I agree with what I said firstly."

"Come on, it's important to be friendly."

"Lemme see." Ruby snatched the phone from her hand. "Meh." she returned it immediately.

Tessa shrugged, too. A friendly conversation was, if nothing else, a positive sign. A relatively significant detail was clear to her. It didn't seem like too much to ask, but guys proved her wrong time and time again. Now, after several hideous attempts to meet the right one, Tessa's standards dropped a notch. Her only aspiration now was normalcy. She hoped to meet someone who wouldn't force her to cringe after each dialogue. She relied on the idea that if the guy was pleasant enough, things would work out somehow.

Ruby pushed the back gate to the office, opening it wide.

"Ha! We're already two minutes late."

●

Tom-the-Friendly had booked a table at June Storm. Most likely, it wasn't his first June Storm date, as he was holding his first voucher. It was crowded, but Tom had arrived on time. He was around Tessa's height and smiled politely. The striped shirt he wore buttoned-up matched with his round glasses, far too big for his face. Shy, but somehow managing to be bold, he invited her inside. As she placed her purse on the couch and tried to adjust to the space, Tom mirrored her across the table.

A glass of wine and a bowl of french fries later — because alcohol and junk were always consumed at lunchtime in this city — Tessa had learned a lot about Tom. She had found out that he had recently been hired by one of the largest social media networks in the world. Whose name we won't mention here for copyright reasons. Tessa also learned that he grew up in a family of maths teachers. That he lived in several countries. Where he felt lonely each time because he didn't speak the language. Now in London, he lived in an apartment where no one locked the front door. Tessa felt that after a series of countless chaotic encounters, she had found someone who could keep up with a good conversation. Tessa told him about the job that was slowly killing her. About her desire to apply for new positions. About her fear of being turned down. And about her neurotic landlady, who was chasing foxes at night. All the while, Tom listened with an endearing smile and a twinkle in his eyes.

"I'm sorry, when I start talking about myself, I fail to stop."

"No, not at all. I'm glad to hear from you." he replied, without losing eye contact.

The place began to get crowded.

"If I may ask you, what was the reason your last relationship ended?"

"Uhm." Tessa thought for a moment. "He seemed way too much like Karl Marx."

"Appearance-wise or the way he was thinking?"

"Thinking, fortunately. I would say."

"Have you ever visited the Highgate Cemetery?" Tom asked all of a sudden, seeming to change the subject; but not really.

"The Highgate Cemetery?"

"Yes. Many famous people were buried there, including Marx." he looked at his wristwatch. "If we leave now, we'll probably arrive just an hour before closing time."

"Why do you think I would like to see Marx's tomb?"

"Because it's fun. It's not far. It's in north London."

"Where did you suddenly get all this information from?"

"I have a lot of information that I would love to share with you."

Tom tossed a bill on the table and pointed at Tessa.

The Highgate Cemetery was surrounded by a fence, through which one could already see inside. Collapsing ancient tombs, perfect for a horror scene. But luckily, there were a few more hours until sunset. Tom insisted on paying for both tickets. Tessa didn't even bother to try to pay. That was not for traditional, feminist reasons necessarily.

"Doesn't it seem ironic to you that you need a ticket to see Marx?" Tessa asked as they both walked down the alley surrounded by tombstones that resembled frivolous mushrooms.

"No. And we don't see Marx. We see a statue."

Even though it was June and the weather was nice, the cemetery was gloomy and sad. Tourists and locals were all turning leaflets from side to side, trying to identify some of the famous graves that were displayed in the photos they held in their hands. Tom pointed to a side path, where the vast majority of tourists seemed to gather.

"In the 1970's, it was said that a vampire, a bloodthirsty entity, haunted this place."

Tessa looked at him, unimpressed.

"Do you believe in vampires?" he spoke, as if asking her if she was religious.

"Sorry, no." she laughed, hoping he was joking.

But Tom then made up his mind that it wasn't the right time for anecdotes anymore, as they had reached the main alley once again. The place resembled a little maze that somehow always brought people back to the big alley. Curious and thoughtful, Tom stood in front of the much-praised statue. He gestured at Tessa not to hesitate to come closer. Tom threw himself into the crowd of tourists that had arrived for photo sessions. He, in turn, strived to produce high-quality panoramic images. An Asian couple was taking selfies by the bronze bust. Tessa squeezed a polite but tormented smile, keeping her distance.

"You know, he wasn't that bad." Tom suddenly said.

"What wasn't bad?"

"The dude. Marx. Years ago in Vietnam, I learned about him at school."

Tessa looked around at other tombstones. Satisfied with the quality of his new photos, Tom packed his phone away.

"Do you want ice cream?"

"I'm glad you're asking. Yes!"

"Then let's get outta here!"

"Sure you don't want a picture with you next to the statue?" she asked, more or less jokingly.

He shook his head and urged her to hurry up.

"If we catch the next bus, we'll get there just in time."

"In time for what?"

"For ice cream."

She struggled to keep up as Tom rushed down the alley towards the main road. It seemed that he had no time to waste. Tessa smiled to herself. She had forgotten how much she resembled Tom in that respect. He reminded her of one side of herself that she had buried in a distant cemetery without even realising it. Brandon was the kind of person who took his time. He wasn't in a hurry when he went for walks, he wasn't in a hurry even when he was late. He kept his laconic and relaxed pace no matter the situation. Tessa had learned to adapt. To go for a walk, not to sprint, in the days when she would've rather run an entire marathon. But Tom was an invigorating change. A reminder of who Tessa was once in the past and who she wanted to be in the future.

The sun was setting over the bus stop and Tom pulled a pack of cigarettes out of his trouser pocket. Sitting on the bench next to him, Tessa tried not to judge, but she couldn't claim to expressly admire his habit.

"Sorry, do you mind if I smoke?"

"Not really."

"Do you want one?" he urged her to help herself.

"No, thank you, I don't smoke."

"Come on, they're Korean cigarettes."

Tessa raised an eyebrow.

"A friend of mine always brings a lot of packages when he comes back from holiday. They're lemon flavoured. They're not too bad! And on top of that, they're free!"

As he eagerly pulled out his lemon cigarette, Tessa stared with melancholy at the hill behind the buildings across the street. In no time, the bus appeared around the corner. Tom jumped to his feet and checked his watch.

"Just in time!" he rejoiced. "Will it be chocolate ice cream?"

Turning her head towards him and examining his nerdy shirt and glasses that covered half of his face, Tessa felt a bizarre air of freedom. She then snatched the lemon-flavoured Korean cigarette from his fingers and sucked, unable to actually smoke, but enjoying the spontaneous gesture itself.

It was dark near Tower Bridge, but the city lights kept the atmosphere awake. Lively passing cars and party people.

"We've crossed the wrong street. We have to get over *there* and then cross the bridge." Tom pointed at the opposite side of the road.

Tessa looked briefly around herself.

"Let's go back then."

Tom stared at her for a moment, not saying a word.

"What...?" she tried to push him to speak.

Taking advantage of the cars now stopped at the traffic light, Tom grabbed Tessa's hand, pulling her across the road against her will. Cars started driving as soon as the lights turned green.

"You're trying to kill me!" Tessa shouted, as Tom burst out laughing.

In spite of herself, Tessa grinned. She was enjoying this streak of cutting loose and being carefree. Knowing that chocolate ice cream was waiting for her on the other side of the road definitely helped. Without being judged. Without being told how unhealthy it was.

Arriving safely, Tessa gently claimed her hand back and Tom didn't argue that. Happiness was clear on her face, but she was still missing something. Something was incomplete.

●

Tom was a good guy. If Tessa decided to make a list of all the qualities she was looking for in a man, Tom would be in the top ten of this ranking. Not like he had a lot of other competitors, but the important part was that Tom was in a good position on that list. When it came to physical appearance, he was not a model, but he was not exactly ugly. He was presentable enough. Nerdy, but nice and interesting.

Now, it is very tempting to judge Tessa. But she always highlighted that physical appearance was never her first bullet point. Paradoxical in this exposition, for sure. But if she were to claim that she was not interested in physical appearance as well, she would be a liar. Tom had a good education, decent social status and a well-paid job. He had a sense of humour, but he never made bad jokes. He was gentle and caring and always had an ear to listen to all the nonsense that went through Tessa's mind. Tom exhibited all these qualities from their first date. At first and even second glance, he was perfect. Moreover, he showed a visible interest in Tessa. Without being naughty and without exceeding any limits.

In conclusion, Tessa was honoured by the attention she received from Tom. It made her feel comfortable, appreciated and protected. Yet, something made her hesitate. She tried to figure out why she felt something was missing when she thought of Tom. It's very true that women don't know what they want and that they're difficult to comprehend. The above exposition validates this point. But at thc samc time, it is also true that women have an innate intuition. As they say, it's usually wise to listen it.

This wasn't just intuition. If Tessa were to describe Tom as an object, then he would be a balloon. Not a helium one. Not a hot-air balloon. A normal party balloon. Colourful, lively, and pleasing to the eye. He was very easy to talk to, as balloons go. She felt that they could drift apart and reconnect after months and still find conversation easy. But while there was a connection, Tessa found it difficult to imagine him as a potential romantic suitor. Although her introspection had come up fairly inconclusive so far, she had at least deduced that she was probably looking for something beyond a friendly balloon. But the night was young.

How's that for an insight into how a woman's brain works in moments of crisis?

Walking to the tube station with Tom, Tessa didn't care whether he wanted to see her again soon or not. Or if he didn't want to see her again at all. The last thought worried her. Of course, she wanted to feel that he was serious about her, but at the same time, she wanted to be left guessing. To feel intrigued.

Tessa was afraid that as soon as she got to know Tom in more detail, she would realise that they weren't a good match. Even though they had a lot in common. Tessa was also aware that she was overthinking; too much, too soon. But this was another trait of hers. These thoughts were analysed and over-analysed within a few seconds. During which time a guy would've admired a passing sports car that he couldn't afford to buy. What frightened Tessa was the thought that, in her mind, she had already placed Tom in the friendzone. Because there she could keep him close to her. Without promising him any romantic relationship, which she couldn't offer him. Not now. And never in the future.

The problem, of course, was not Tom. But neither was it Tessa. It was simply not a good romantic match. If she were to describe him to her friends, she would present him as the ideal man she had always hoped to meet. Somewhere deep inside though, she felt that he was too good to her.

There was no point to discuss how women are attracted only to men who treat them badly. In this situation, it was clear that Tessa wanted him to be nice to her. But at the same time, to keep his masculine qualities. Tessa didn't want to feel dominated. But she didn't want to feel that she had a stronger, even more masculine personality compared to his. Rather, Tessa wanted someone sensitive but strong in character. Not stubborn, but not too soft either. Tessa felt like Tom was inclined to approve of every idea of hers. To smile at every word of hers. To tell her she was right even when she herself would contradict herself. Tessa didn't want a companion to constantly contradict her. But she wanted someone who could debate with her. Someone who had his opinions, which he was not afraid to express without offending her. Tessa wanted him not to be afraid to contradict her when she was wrong.

We could say now that Tessa had judged Tom after only a few hours spent together. Anyone now would say that Tessa was in a hurry to make a decision about their future together. Or far from each other; and that all her thoughts now sounded like she was preparing to escape from her own wedding.

Walking into the tube station, Tom followed Tessa down the escalator.

"Are we going in the same direction?" she asked.

"Not really."

"Didn't you say you're taking the bus?"

"Yes."

"Why are you going down to the tube station then?"

Tom shrugged.

"I'm walking you there."

"Did you just pay for a journey just to walk me to the platform?"

"It's almost midnight. I would feel guilty to leave you here alone."

Grateful, Tessa smiled. The train stopped at the station and Tom motioned for Tessa to hurry.

"Thanks for today. It was a pleasant walk through the cemetery."

"Anytime."

He hugged her affectionately.

"Now hurry up."

Tessa hopped in.

"I hope to see you again soon," he added.

Tessa replied with a friendly smile; and here's what sealed the future. She sat down on a chair, waving back at him. Friendly. As the doors closed, Tom was still standing on the platform, answering with the same gesture, glad to be able to say goodnight.

"Message me when you get home." he added, pointing at his phone.

Tessa approved and made it clear that he could leave now, not wanting to hold him back any longer. The train hadn't left yet and

Tessa waved at him once more, that she was fine. He assured her that he didn't mind watching her train leave. It started to catch speed. Tom waved goodbye again. Tessa smiled as her view went dark. She was grateful for her new connection. Impressed in a positive way with the first person who didn't bring her to the depths of her despair.

But she felt as if she had turned into a balloon herself. She felt empty inside. Like a balloon in the corner of a room. On a birthday party without guests. Who had all promised in one form or another, to show up, but never did.

While Tessa was trying, and hoping, to keep her composure and analytical skills, Ruby had chosen a more aggressive approach when it came to her ex-boyfriend. It was the same clear June night in west London and the perfect night for Ruby and her planned attacks. Equipped and filled with a destructive appetite, she sneaked among the expensive cars parked in front of some familiar buildings. Surveillance cameras were facing away, covering insignificant corners. For unknown reasons and to Ruby's satisfaction, all the cars were left unattended.

She had to be quick. To make sure she didn't waste time, she rushed to pull a screwdriver out of her purse and aimed it at Arif's car. She walked from one end to the other, making sure she scraped the enamel of Arif's beloved property.

"Take this, sucker!"

Standing by the hood, Ruby admired her work.

"A piece of art."

She wasn't sure if she still loved Arif, but she certainly missed him. She hated him. At least that's what she thought. She didn't want to see him again, but also, she couldn't live without him. Arif was a big part of her life and would always be, she felt. She couldn't imagine a life away from him. If she couldn't make him still love her, she hoped she could at least arouse any other feelings inside him. Even if those were of anger or hate. Ruby hated Arif and she was disgusted with herself that she was so attached to him. When she wasn't with him, she didn't know how to organise her own life. She felt that she had no purpose. The days were long, boring and aimless.

"At least when we were together, I had someone to wait for at home every evening," she said, still looking at his car.

Ruby wanted Arif next to her more so she wouldn't feel alone. She knew she was afraid of loneliness. Arif, for better or worse, brought her relief. It gave her a purpose and made her feel useful. Ruby wanted that scratch to be the connection between the two of them. She wanted to make it clear to him that they couldn't live away from each other. Ruby hoped that feeling was mutual.

●

Tessa slowly declared herself slightly desperate.

She had a significant number of people in her inbox. Some wrote her messages, invited her into town, or made various proposals to her. Some were rather disturbing while others were plain and boring. However, Tessa didn't feel flattered at all.

"Quality, not quantity," she repeated to herself all the time. Contrary to Ruby's belief that she was on the exact opposite path. She had come to contradict herself because she had found quality: Tom. So here was the problem. If someone quality like Tom made her feel like a sad and deflated balloon, then what was she really looking for?

All these thoughts made her feel confused. Tessa now felt a desperate need to meet as many people as possible. To meet the opposite sex. To compare them with each other. She had to know the quality ones. People like Tom. But not Tom. Something like this. Tessa was looking for someone who was kind, polite, funny, intelligent and respectful. She was looking for someone who would listen to her, but someone who had stories to tell. Someone who would keep her company late into the night. To chat about conspiracy theories and supermarket discounts. Tessa wanted a Tom, but a Tom that made her feel fulfilled. So Liam appeared.

He looked like a child. He wasn't exactly a baby, but he was still a student and a year younger than Tessa. Liam listened to the same music as Tessa, laughed at the same jokes and shared the same sense of humour. He even appreciated her sometimes occasional hints of dark humour.

Liam was a student who worked part-time at a finance company. His work was often very tedious. He had to enter numbers into an excel file. He compared his career to modern slavery. But once he finished his studies, he would occupy a much more interactive position, so to speak.

He had a tight budget and lived a hungry student life, despite his job. He was used to pouring ketchup over spaghetti and eating that for three days in a row for dinner. He was only able to afford a few drinks with colleagues in town on Friday nights. This behaviour of his entered Tessa's life like a warm summer breeze. A fresh and playful June wind.

Liam sometimes talked about his stepfather who had adopted him at the age of seven. At other times, he avoided any serious discussion and waited for Tessa and her daily dose of memes. For several days, Tessa didn't know what she could think of him. But she knew for sure that his presence guaranteed her amusement and levity. She had found someone who fully appreciated her jokes, making her feel like a quality stand-up comedian. She had always known that she was much funnier than most of the men she had met. But it gave her strength to know someone who appreciated her sense of humour and recognised it in front of her.

And with that, another feeling crept into this connection. Namely, the desire to protect him. Like an older sister. Here's the problem again. In one form or another, Tessa felt that this feeling was mutual by the way he behaved. He didn't ever take the initiative other than to spend quality time together, having fun over various insignificant topics.

Sitting on the steps in Trafalgar Square just before midnight — at the place where strangers bonded, friendships fell apart and alcohol was consumed — the wind became cool. Liam was wearing only a T-shirt and was shaking.

"You're cold."

"No." he replied. "I had a great time today."

"I'm not contradicting you, but I still think you're cold."

"Okay. Just a little bit," he admitted, pulling his arms through the sleeves of his shirt, trying to keep his warmth under his shirt. "This helps."

"Do you wanna leave? I'd say we call it a day."

"No. I like it here. I want to stay."

Tessa wanted to give him a jacket and put it over his shoulders. But she didn't have one. Like a caring mother, she wanted to protect him. This confirmed what Tessa knew from the beginning.

"It's like you're a long-lost brother. I feel like we've met before in another lifetime. And we were brothers."

"Ha! If you say so." he laughed.

A group of three drunk guys ran down the stairs, shouting indecipherable words as they headed for the fountain.

"I'll jump! Naked! Wanna see? Wanna film?" they shouted at each other.

Still trembling, Liam watched them and shook his head.

"Kids these days." he sighed.

One of these young men turned to Liam and pointed a finger at him.

"I see you."

Then, observing Tessa, he framed them both into a rectangle made of four fingers, holding a cinematic frame in front of his eyes.

"You two are soulmates. Please get married!" exclaimed the guy, then ran to the fountain, wondering whether or not it was worth a dip in the cold midnight waters.

It is said that only the child and the drunk man tell the truth. If this was indeed destiny, Tessa had one more reason to feel confused.

CHAPTER FIVE

The phones rang. Keyboards clicked. Rebecca answered a call while loudly munching on some gum. Ruby was trying to move her chair to an angle where Philip couldn't see her applying her morning facial routine. The perfume she was applying to her neck gave her away. Philip tilted his head from behind the monitor. Ruby pulled her chair back to where it should have been from the beginning and opened an email to pretend she was reading. Then she looked at her phone to see if she had received any new notifications. Disappointed, she turned her attention back to work.

"Yeah, my name is Rebecca" she sighed, still talking on the phone. "It's spelled 'Rebecca' with a single 'c', only in my case it has two 'c's'. Exactly. Can I help you with anything else?"

Ruby glanced at Tessa.

"News?"

"Nah. Nothing fascinating."

Ruby's phone told her she had a call on hold. She reluctantly pressed the receiver and leaned back in her chair.

"Ruby speaking. How can I help you?" She then muted the call. "But you said you were going on a date! Nothing came from there?"

"Found only friendships. It's a pretty miserable situation."

"Mmm. Dang!" Ruby turned her microphone on again. "Sorry, the line's cutting off. Can you repeat that again, please?"

Tessa also took a call.

"Tessa speaking. How can I help you?" She then also muted the call. “I'm telling you it's awful! But what's even worse is that I lost all the excitement I still had in me…”

“You don't need enthusiasm. All you need is patience… We certainly didn't lose your booking, sir. If you let me know your booking number once again, maybe we'll find it.”

“Well, I also lost my enthusiasm for patience… If you want to bring your children, you have to book a bigger room.”

Suddenly, the fire alarm went off. Philip jumped, all worked up.

“It's "Rebecca", just like ‘Rebeca’, only that it's written ‘Rebecca’, if you understand what I'm saying.” Rebecca muttered, spreading the chewing gum between her fingers and teeth until it was way too long and too cold to put back into her mouth, so she threw it into the bin. “Yes. I think there's a fire in our office. I think it’ll soon be too dangerous to keep talking to you on the phone.”

Tessa and Ruby ended their calls. Fiona stood up as if awakened from the dead.

“Let's hurry towards the fire exit!” Philip exclaimed.

“Do I have time to grab a coffee?”

“No, Ruby, there’s no time for coffee!” Slightly irritated, Philip had to raise his voice, to make himself heard.

“Fine…”

The fire alarm was deafeningly annoying.

“No problem, I can stay on the line. I’ll let you know when it gets too hot.” Rebecca continued.

“Rebecca, we’re leaving!” insisted Philip.

Fiona hugged her purse and favourite desk decorations and ran towards the door. The team followed her.

Compared to the air conditioning in the office, the sun was overwhelming. Almost instantly, firefighters parked in front of the building, to put out a non-existent fire. It was a false alarm. Tessa looked at her watch. She had two hours left until the end of her shift. A flame lit up inside her chest. A few dark clouds then gathered over the office buildings, as if preparing to quench the fire in Tessa's heart. The atmosphere was stifling, but in a positive way. The thought immediately led her to where she wanted to spend her evening as soon as she was free to leave.

June Storm. Several people were enjoying their cocktails on the corner sofa. Tonight, the atmosphere was soothing, with hints of scented candles and mystery in the air. Alcohol bottles gleamed at the bar. Colin greeted Tessa with a smile and she sat down in front of him. Over her shoulder, she then noticed a familiar presence. His face was half-shaded, but Tessa still recognised him by his iconic hairstyle.

"You!"

"Good evening." Nev bowed his head to greet the only young lady in the salon.

"Merlot?" Colin asked.

"Please."

"And a glass of water for me." Nev told the bartender, then gestured at Tessa for permission to sit next to her.

"I'm starting to think there's something weird going on here, because we run into each other by accident way too often. Don't you think so?" Tessa said, watching his water being poured while Nev took a seat on the bar stool.

"The only unearthly phenomenon here is your desire to see me again, milady." Nev replied, leaning back slightly to admire her in more detail.

"What do you mean?"

"Be honest. You wanted me to be here."

"Why would I want that? I don't even know you well enough."

"You certainly have your justification. A reason of yours."

"What reason? I have no hidden agenda."

"I didn't mean a hidden agenda. I said, reasons. You wanted to talk to me. You planned it in your head and now it's become reality."

"Maybe. I've felt alone. I came here hoping to have a conversation."

"Consequently, your wish is fulfilled. So enjoy!" he smiled playfully and slightly sarcastic, but honest.

Colin placed the red wine in front of Tessa and the glass of water next to Nev. Tessa looked at Nev and didn't know what to say, for something aroused her curiosity.

"Pay attention to the words, thoughts and feelings you carry with you. They are all thrown into the Universe, from where they bounce back into your life in the form of actions."

Nev then swallowed the plain water in one gulp.

"I don't think it has anything to do with how cautious I am. It's about those around me. I'm afraid I only meet people I don't want."

"Are we speaking about romantic dates here?"

"Indeed."

"Well, you're not going to get rid of what you're afraid of. You will attract it. So what are you afraid of?"

"I'm not afraid of things like these." Tessa laughed, still a little embarrassed. "I only set out some time ago to accomplish a few things, to meet certain people." she added, taking a sip of wine. "But if I think about it, I don't particularly insist on these things happening. I'm fine just the way I am now."

"It seems to me that your mind is troubled."

Nev called Colin and asked him to bring another glass of water.

"Why do you always have to have an answer to everything?"

Instantly receiving another glass of water, Nev pushed it in front of Tessa and urged her to drink. Colin withdrew again, not wanting to appear nosy, but curiosity gnawed at him.

"I didn't ask for water. It's yours."

"No, it's for you." Nev smiled confidently. "Drink it up, milady. We need the glass. Also, staying hydrated has never hurt anyone."

Tessa carried out the order, leaving the empty glass back on the counter.

"You're a magnet, milady."

"You're the magnet! You always show up wherever I am."

"I'm wherever your thoughts are."

"Don't try to hit on me, you're not my type." she stated, pointing at Nev and sipping at her wine.

Nev then urged her to hold the glass. The sunglasses hanging from the second button of his shirt flickered briefly as he grabbed her hands. Tessa lost herself in the moment.

"Now imagine the perfect reality in which you want to live. The new people you meet, the special experiences you have."

A few candles in the corner of the pub went out. Their aroma gradually spread throughout the room. Colin went to replace them.

"Why?" Tessa asked, looking for Nev's gaze.

"Just imagine. Live that moment. Now."

"You're confusing me. You're putting too much pressure on me!"

"Milady." he accentuated, gripping both her wrists. "If your ideal person were to walk through the door right now, what would they look like?"

"Ideal." Tessa whispered after a short hesitation.

"Be more specific, I beg you."

Tessa tried to avoid the clichés of any romantic comedy, but she could still feel Nev's touch across the back of her hand, even though he had already let go of her.

"Polite? Educated? Handsome, I suppose."

"Be more specific."

"Brown hair? Of average height?"

"I need details." he insisted, his voice still soft.

"Why are you forcing me to do this? I don't understand."

"Stated, in detail."

"Wealthy! American! Wearing a blue T-shirt. Is that enough for you?"

"Of course, that sounds better." Nev smiled, straightening his back in satisfaction.

Tessa puffed irritated, avoiding his gaze in order to calm down. The last customers were now leaving for home. It wasn't even that late.

"I think I'm sorry that I let you listen to my private issues. I see you're laughing at me now."

"On the contrary, milady. Today I help you open a door to a world of unlimited possibilities."

"Sounds exciting."

"Now envision."

"What?"

"Everything you said earlier. Except for the part where you blamed me for laughing at you. Come on. Try it."

At first, Tessa hesitated. Then she closed her eyes. Colin had just managed to light the new candles. The three seemed to be in a cult hidden away from the world. Tessa meditated on her ideals, her aspirations. Envisioning the future, as if it were the present. Joy suddenly flooded her soul. She opened her eyes. Nev was still there, motionless. The expression on his face now had no expectation on her part. Tessa felt fulfilled and relieved, so she smiled. After this short imaginary journey, Nev helped her pour her wine into the empty glass.

"Bottoms up!"

"It's wine!" she protested.

"Bottoms up!"

Tessa carried out the order, putting the empty glass back on the counter.

"It's your reality. You're living it right now." Nev nodded approvingly.

"What did you have before coming here?" Tessa then looked at Colin. "What did you give him?"

A thunder sounded at once and torrential rain began straight after. The wind brought a few twigs and leaves through the open door. Raindrops hit the bar counter.

"Why does it always rain when I see you?" Tessa asked then, resting her chin on her palm to examine Nev more at length.

"It's raining because you always leave home without an umbrella, milady. And I always have a spare."

Tessa stared at the open door, the warm rain beginning to touch her arm. Nev lit some cannabis and his iconic laughter reappeared. Tessa shook her hand to clean the air.

"You know these are going to kill you one day."

"One day, milady." he shrugged. "But that day is not today."

●

That same evening, Tessa sat amongst the empty seats on the Central Line and smiled to herself. A feeling of well-being and positive anticipation ensued as the tube rushed underground. No expectations. A clear mind. Just a state of affirmative abundance.

Nev leaned his back against a side wall in Chinatown, a cigarette hanging between his fingers. His gaze was clouded as the smoke he exhaled caressed his cheekbones. Noisy passers-by were now just an echo in his imagination. His senses gradually abandoned him. Today he opened a door to a new existence for yet another person. To the realm he discovered. That he was so proud of; he wanted the whole world to be aware of the secret he held. The kindness that existed in Nev made him smile at the thought that he had helped someone discover answers that had been floating in the Universe forever. At the same time, he was aware of his own degradation from which he didn't want to escape. As

Tessa sped towards new horizons, Nev consciously sank into his own misery. He smiled as raindrops dripped from the roof under which he was hiding.

•

Late for work, Tessa hurried out of her room, putting shoes on while trying to unlock the door. Imo appeared from the living room, pulling unhappily at the white T-shirt he was wearing.

"Hey, T, do you know if there's a problem with the washing machine?"

Tessa tied her laces.

"No, why?"

"In my opinion, my shirt got stained."

She looked up to see the blue stains on his previously immaculate T-shirt.

"I don't know, Imo, maybe you're using too much detergent. I'm in a rush now."

"Hm." he scratched the back of his neck, then shrugged. "Possible."

Tessa picked her purse up and ran down the street. The door closed loudly behind her, causing a moment of hesitation. Nevertheless, she remembered that she was late, so immediately ran towards the tube station.

The road to the office was crowded and hectic, as usual. A bus was trying to pass, but the crowd cut off its way. A stranger was waiting on the other side of the boulevard, preoccupied with his phone. Tessa couldn't help but notice the blue striped shirt he was wearing, because it looked like a zebra, only more aquatic. Another young man stopped next to him, holding a briefcase close to his chest, somewhat panicked that someone would steal it. A navy blue briefcase. The bus finally managed to get out of the way, so Tessa crossed. A group of loud students in azure uniforms got in her way. One of them pushed the other, and he collided with Tessa.

"Sorry," he said, before rejoining his friends.

"It's all right." she replied, glancing at her watch.

A few athletes walked out of a gym. Dressed from head to toe in blue T-shirts.

"Or maybe it isn't all right."

At the office, Tessa tossed her purse on the chair and hurriedly turned her computer on.

"All good? All good? The usual?" Ruby almost sang, rocking her chair a few times.

"No. I think something weird's going on."

"Did recruiters reach out to you?" Ruby whispered. "Are you resigning?"

"I see people dressed in blue."

"Sorry, what?"Tessa pushed her chair towards Ruby and began to speak in a low voice for fear of being misinterpreted.

"You know the guy I told you about. The one who keeps bumping into me."

"No, I don't know what guy keeps bumping into you." Ruby replied, becoming slightly critical of Tessa.

"The chain smoker. The wanna-be actor."

"No, Tessa, you lost me. But you know I have a bad memory. So yeah, maybe you told me about him."

"Anyway. Listen to this. I was in *June Storm* yesterday."

"You've been, where?"

"My favourite pub in town."

"Since when do you have a favourite pub? What did I miss?"

Tessa thought for a moment, realising that she had spoken without further analysis of what was happening to her. She had found a new social circle, a new refuge, but she hadn't explicitly felt the need to lay it all out so far.

"I'll explain later. What is for sure is that he was there too. Again, by coincidence."

"Aha. I'm not sure I'm quite following. But what you're trying to say now is that there is no such thing as a coincidence."

"No, that's not what I'm trying to say. The point is, he proposed something stupid last night. At least that's what I thought at first."

"What did he propose? You two naughty little "

"To pour liquid from one glass to another and imagine something from my future."

"Uhm. Right. And what did you imagine?"

"A man dressed in blue."

"Wait, what?"

"I know, I know. That's after he annoyed me with too many questions about how I would describe my ideal man."

"He asked you to describe your ideal man, and out of all the traits you could come up with, you decided on a man dressed in blue?"

"You're not listening! The problem is… Whatever that was last night, I thought it was a joke. But it looks like something's afoot today. I've walked past a couple of dozen people dressed in blue at least, just on the way here!"

Ruby leaned closer to Tessa.

"What did you say he's smoking? Did you have some too?"

"I didn't smoke anything! How would you explain this story?"

"Uhm, maybe it's Blue Shirt Day?"

"That's in October."

"Earth Day, but they're dressed in blue to celebrate our melting glaciers?"

"Why would melting glaciers be celebrated?"

"I don't know, Tessa."

"And no, that's in April."

"I don't know, Tessa, I really don't know."

"That's what I thought too." she sighed at last, returning to her desk.

"You need a holiday. Urgently. That's for sure."

"Don't make me laugh! If I ask for days off now, he'll approve them by the end of the year."

"You can try. What have you got to lose?"

Tessa shrugged, focusing on her inbox flooded with emails waiting for an answer. But leaving work aside for a moment, Tessa pressed an unread notification in the corner of her screen. Philip asked her to fill out the days for which she wanted to have holidays. Paranoid, Tessa stood up to look for Philip. He was not in the office. She then sat down again.

"Can I choose my days off?" she wrote to the seemingly ubiquitous manager, who replied immediately with a message.

"Please choose them today. I have to pass the list on. Please take them this month if possible."

"You're kidding!" she typed back. "That's not how this company works."

"Well, it's not like it suits me. The order came from my own manager."

Tessa's nose twitched. It's not as if she was bothered by this.

"Are you saying I can be off on Monday?"

"You would do me a great favour if you took all ten days off at once. That way I can group each of you now in the summer and get you back in full formation for the coming autumn, when we have more work to do. If you enter the data now, I can approve it until after lunch."

Theatrically, Tessa turned her chair to face Ruby and then grinned. Ruby looked at her, almost startled.

"What?!"

Tessa shrugged, unable to wipe the smile from her face. She had no idea what she was going to do with two unexpected weeks off, but one thing was clear: she was going to be away from the office.

Tessa tossed her shoes at the front door. As she hung her keys up, Imo danced into view, raising a brochure in both hands.

"Guess who won a holiday in Ibiza?" he sang, gesturing extravagantly.

"I don't know, Pope Francis?"

"I did, T, I did!"

"On what occasion?" Tessa asked, walking to the kitchen for a glass of water.

"I got this voucher in exchange for a gaming voucher. I know, I also thought it was weird of me. Then I thought I had won the jackpot. A free holiday, man! Hotel and two meals a day. Plane tickets. Two weeks, starting Monday. A jackpot!"

He paused, the smile fading from his face.

"That sounds great, doesn't it?"

"Yeah, it does. The thing is, I'm not allowed to take days off."

"Oh." Tessa frowned.

"And the guy doesn't wanna give me the gaming thing back."

"Understandable…"

"Yeah, never mind." he gestured. "Maybe I'll put them up for sale."

"That's kind of illegal, isn't it?" asked Tessa, crossing the hall to retreat in her bedroom.

"Somewhat. I would give it to you. But I know that stupid

company you work for doesn't even give you one paid day off. If I didn't get it, you never will."

"I know, right?" Tessa laughed.

"Yeah man, see you later. I've got some games to win."

Tessa stopped in the doorway. It took her a few seconds. But she then turned back to face Imo, who was waving around a free vacation between his fingers.

CHAPTER SIX

Tessa owed Imo. A lot. As evening approached, she placed her suitcase at her feet and looked up at the hotel. She had to take a step back in order to admire in more detail the lair that would be hers for the next two weeks. No one but Imo, of course, knew where Tessa was going to spend her spontaneous vacation. For her own peace at the office, this trip would remain a secret for the time being. Ibiza was not necessarily on the list of priorities in Tessa's life, but this free trip was not exactly to be denied. Tessa picked up her suitcase and walked up the stairs.

The hotel was five stars, an experience that Tessa would be unlikely to be able to afford under normal circumstances at any point in her lifetime. Despite this, it had a fairly modest entrance in size. The glass ornaments created an optical illusion that gave the place a spacious effect. The beach could be seen right through the large window next to the reception desk.

Tessa had a voucher in her wallet, which allowed her free access to her room and two meals a day. The package also included a welcome cocktail of her choice. She unpacked her suitcase once she arrived in her room and changed into a modest evening dress. And because no one would refuse drinks on the house, Tessa made her way to the restaurant and bar downstairs.

Seeing the expensive watches some tourists were wearing, Tessa pushed her voucher underneath her purse, wanting to make it disappear from her eyesight. Still seeing a corner of the hidden voucher, she noticed that it was sponsored by June Storm. Tessa narrowed her eyes, only now reading the small inscription. The restaurant was decorated with Mediterranean plants. Several couples dined at tables by the window or sat at the bar. Larger families had their own corner, where their children could jump around without being too much of a nuisance.

And then there was Tessa. She planted herself onto a small sofa, as if it were made for a single person. It was getting dark outside and the sensor lights were starting to light up. A young employee was walking from table to table to light candles. Tessa took a deep breath, trying to enjoy how the negative energy was drained from her body. Or so she hoped. Holidays were meant to relieve the body of stress and daily worries. At least, that's what she just read on the cover of the magazine that was lying next to her on the couch. Just then, a tray appeared above her table.

“Unfortunately, we don't have any Long Island today. But here's a Blue Lagoon on the house as an apology.”

Tessa looked up. Next to her stood a smiling, dark-haired young man of average height. But the first detail that stood out that Tessa couldn’t omit was his American accent.

“Uhm, thanks.” Tessa replied, taking the glass. She immediately had to put it down, as it was so cold that her hand almost clung to it.

“When you're ready to order again, my friend Antonio is all eyes and ears." he said, pointing at the young bartender who was busy sipping from a drink after preparing it at the bar. “I don't work here.”

“Oh.” was the only sound Tessa was able to make.

“Okay. Listen.” He took a deep breath, ready to say whatever he had to say in one piece, and then to leave. “You've been drawing my friend's attention, but because he's too shy to start a conversation, I've decided to take the initiative and relieve him of his suffering.”

Tessa glanced at Antonio and noticed the talent with which he shook the ice.

“Long Island is of course on the menu and if it's not too much trouble, he'd be happier to serve you straight at the bar. Until then, enjoy this cocktail, it's on him. I'm gonna head out now.”

“Thanks!” Tessa said in the first instance, to somehow make this stranger stay with her for another second.

For one reason or another, Tessa enjoyed this short conversation like none before. Despite the fact that she herself had only contributed to 20% of the dialogue.

"See you around." he said, picking up his tray and ready to leave.

"Hey!" Tessa raised her voice, wanting to hold him back for another moment. "Are you American?"

"So the accent gave me away. There's nothing I can do, unfortunately." he laughed. "See you later." he concluded, waving his hand.

Tessa smiled. The next second, she was alone in her corner again. Sipping from her cocktail, she scrolled through the dating app and avoided a few annoying messages that made her roll her eyes. Then she looked up at Antonio, who immediately took his eyes off her. Tessa packed her bag and headed for the bar. Antonio noticed her initiative and pretended to be busy. Tessa knew she had nothing to lose and she couldn't fail any worse than she already had during her previous dates.

"Hi!" she said, taking a seat.

Antonio flinched, his hands continuing to work. He decided to look for his brush to clean his wine glasses.

"Thanks for the cocktail."

Antonio smiled briefly, but avoided her gaze. There was silence between the two. Only a few children were yelling and running somewhere in the background.

"I hope I didn't misunderstand," she spoke then, wanting to kill the silence, but also slightly paranoid. "You sent this over, right?"

"I did... But the initiative was Dean's."

"Dean?"

"The guy who served you...?"

"The one who doesn't work here."

"That's right." Antonio approved.

Tessa nodded gratefully. Another prolonged moment of awkward silence.

"So the idea was yours or Dean's?"

"The idea was mine, Dean's initiative."

"Nice of you two."

The children couldn't help but go crazy in the background. Several couples sat down at secluded tables.

"This hotel is nice. A little expensive." Tessa found herself talking, just to fill the empty and awkward silence. "Slightly over my budget, but there are vouchers for that." she laughed, pulling out hers and fluttering it in front of Antonio's nose. "I wouldn't normally admit this to a stranger, but you're employed here, so you'd find out anyway."

"I finish my shift at ten, so in an hour and a half. Do you want to go to the beach after that?"

Finally a reaction.

"Perfect! That gives me enough time to use my dinner voucher tonight!"

•

The beach seemed to only come to life after the darkness had set in. Both tourists who had spent the whole day in the sun and those who hid from the heat inside pubs now crowded the seaside. The local bars got richer every second. Music roared from all speakers, so that songs got messed up in a meaningless remix. But the idea was there. Tourists liked it. A few campfires appeared sporadically. The early party people already spilled their internal excess liquid into the Mediterranean. People were having fun.

"So you're from one of these English countries too." Antonio said, carefully avoiding the partygoers, as if they had scabies or another infectious disease.

"Uhm, yes." Tessa replied, stepping through the still-hot sand. "I live in London. Have you ever visited England?"

"No. I don't go to rainy countries. They make me sick."

"Oh. But it doesn't always rain there. We also have very hot days."

"I can't enjoy hot days when I know that another gloomy and endless period of light rain is coming."

"Oh."

Tessa noticed a not-so-crowded campfire and pointed at it. Antonio examined it, then ignored her proposal.

"Smoke is choking my lungs. It's too hot there. I need more air. Some wind."

“Do you want us to sit closer to the shore?”

Antonio shook his head.

“It's too wet there.”

“Oh.”

Tessa scratched her forehead, realising that she was gradually running out of ideas. It seemed like she was unsuccessfully doing a males’ job. How the tables turn sometimes.

“What brings you to our lands?” he asked robotically.

“Well, as you can see.” Tessa laughed. “I won a voucher and my company finally allowed me to take some leave and —”

“You like ice cream?” he interrupted her suddenly, after he hadn’t even listened to the answer to the first question.

“I do. Where do you think we find the best —”

“What do you think about British politicians?”

“Uhm, if they like ice cream, or do you wanna know about my political views?” Tessa asked, somewhat confused.

“Are you in a relationship?”

“I’m not. Are you?”

“No, the idea of a relationship makes me anxious.”

“Oh.”

“What is your occupation?” he then asked, without looking at his conversation partner. His eyes focused on the path forward, as he had drunk people to avoid.

“I work for a company that —”

“I study psychology. I'm planning on becoming a therapist.” Antonio interrupted her.

“Oh. What kind of therapist exactly?”

“I'm in my last year now. Then I can move to Africa.”

“Africa?”

“They need doctors there quite a bit and I think I'll be useful. I think the competition here in Europe is too fierce. I won't find my place.”

The music was at its peak right now. Antonio had to raise his voice to make himself heard.

“I taught myself French. It's a very beautiful language. Complicated, but accessible in my case. I made a calculation. Most likely I'll move next year. South Africa is my main target, but it's not locked in yet. What do you think about child labor?”

“Uhm, wow. Brutal change of subject! Uhm…”

"I think the British contributed to the latter. All these English colonies! But you're not English, or are you?"

"Well, to be more precise, my great-grandfather was a Jew…"

"I think you're nice!" he exclaimed suddenly. He quickened his pace and Tessa cared not to be left behind. "You're not very talkative, but I don't mind. I learned in class that less talkative people are smarter. Of course, I can't bet on it. But I don't think it would bother me either if you weren't smart. At least you're beautiful. They also taught us in class that good-looking people tend to be more mischievous. It's kind of related to high self-esteem. Society encourages cosmetic treatments and surgeries of all sorts. It's a whole industry."

"Listen!" It was Tessa's turn to interrupt him. "I think you've offended me and humanity enough tonight."

"I believe that many young people of our generation are not ready to receive criticism. They —"

"You!" she raised her voice. "Learn to listen! They don't teach you that in class?"

Antonio looked at Tessa and they both stopped walking. Antonio looked her in the eye for the first time, but without saying a word. Then, without showing any noticeable emotion or facial expression, he ran away, throwing sand at her with his slippers after each step. For the next second, there was silence around Tessa despite the music was still screaming from all the speakers. Perhaps she had been too harsh. But the moment of silence was nice.

●

A relatively familiar shadow could be seen from behind a campfire, right by the shore.

"You!" exclaimed Tessa, quickening her pace without thinking twice.

Leaning on one elbow, Dean sat in solitude, admiring the waves. Seeing Tessa, he gave her a friendly smile.

"You!" she said again, not knowing what to say.

"We met earlier today, didn't we?" he asked, sitting up.

"You have a hell of a friend!" she spoke, letting her anger out on Dean, who narrowed his eyes, slightly confused.

"Ah, did you manage to talk to Antonio after all?"

"Yes! We went on a date just now."

"Was it good?" Dean got excited.

"Did the way I've just approached you seem like I've had a great time?"

"No, not really. Sorry. Antonio can take some getting used to."

"Yeah, I got that feeling all right."

"We're not really friends. We exchanged a few words at the bar today and I noticed that he was watching you, but he was too shy to talk. So I thought I'd give him a hand."

"Please stop playing Cupid from now on. You might be good at other things, but this isn't one of them."

"I promise, I'll step aside from now on."

"The more people I meet, the more I realise that I know nothing about them or about homo sapiens in general."

Dean's smile turned into laughter. Tessa chuckled, too, and her face lit up.

"Do you wanna sit down?" he asked, making room for her next to him.

That night, Tessa learned that Dean was on a pilgrimage through Europe. He was originally from Denver but had also lived in New Orleans for a while. He had started his education somewhere in Chicago. But he wasn't exactly precise when it came to details. He was currently able to study online for his final year, so he decided to travel at the same time. He came from a mixed family and had a sister and a brother. The parents were also in Europe at the moment, but sometimes they went on delegations through South Asia. Dean had been in Ibiza for about two months. He wasn't sure how long he could stay, as he was always looking for new adventures. He spoke only one language but was open to exploring new cultures and learning European customs.

"How about you?" he asked, realising that he had been talking non-stop for some time.

"I work in a call centre in London, but I think I've already specified that."

"The part with London, yes, not the part with the call centre. But how's it going?"

"Pretty generic."

"Generic?"

"Well, like any other call centre. You get call after call... after call. One loony after the other. You end one call in which an aunty from the third floor shouts at you. Even though you're not to blame and she knows that too, she keeps pouring insults into your face. You start another call with someone who doesn't even know why they called. But they blame you for existing. And these are just one category."

Tessa was oblivious to the fact that her tone was getting more and more frustrated. "The category of those who call you, just because they need to vent their anger on another human being. Some kind of free therapy. A one-way street. Because they never listen to what you have to say. It doesn't even matter. Because they call you only to have a monologue. While shouting. Calm people are rare. Then, after you finish a call, if you're lucky and no one else calls, a stack of emails awaits you. Which requires an answer before the end of your shift. And I'm not done yet. You have three different categories of emails. All of which expire at different times, depending on your priority. There is also a chat channel, but I think mine's broken. Because I never receive chats. But I won't let my manager know. If they don't notice, I'm fine as I am. Oh, and speaking of management: disaster. I'm not saying he's not a nice guy. He is. But the whole company is upside down. It's a tragedy. I'm sorry about them. But in the end, I'm more sorry for myself. Sometimes I feel like hitting something!" she exclaimed, clenching her right fist. "I feel like hitting a desk, like this!" she continued, slapping the sand a few times until a few pebbles clung to the edge of her palm. "I feel like breaking the monitor too, but I know I don't have the money to pay for the damage, so I refrain. But I got stress balls. They don't help though. Maybe one day I'll throw them into someone's face. It remains to be seen."

Dean smiled as Tessa detailed her presentation. Then he snorted with laughter.

"Looks like someone got you very upset at work."

Tessa shrugged, slightly embarrassed in front of this stranger, realising that she had shared too many irrelevant details about her daily life. She knew he had every right not to care about her manifesto, but she felt the need to unload in front of someone who was really listening.

“So let me understand. You hate your current job.”

“What’s to like about it?!” Tessa snapped without thinking, not wanting to sound aggressive, for the rage this discussion evoked wasn't even brought by Dean.

“I was just asking.”

“Sorry.” she muttered, wishing with all her heart that she could withdraw at least half of all that she had listed above, for everything could be summed up in a sentence or two.

“What if you could choose? What would you like to do? Where would you like to work?”

Tessa didn't think about it at all.

“To be honest, I don't know. I think all I want now is to leave this company. To be as far away from it as possible. Any other field would be better than the chaos I have to go back to every morning.”

“I hear you.” Dean nodded his head.

As the waves receded, again and again, the tourists packed up one by one. The music faded gradually, until silence settled onto the beach. Only darkness and the sound of waves remained.

●

Tessa opened her eyes to see a clear sky above her and feel the sun already burning her skin. Waking up from her sleep, she sat up, realising that she had fallen asleep on the beach. Dean also woke up, swallowing the sand Tessa had spread on his face as she flinched.

“Shit!” she exclaimed, immediately touching her pockets to make sure she had all her belongings.

She had fallen asleep on the beach, that was clear. But why she hadn't woken up even once during the night was less explicable. Dean wiped the gunk from his eyes as if he wasn’t doing this for the first time. Shame seized Tessa. Not as if she had committed a crime, but more because she had been vulnerable to a stranger. It was one thing to fall asleep on the tube on the way to the office, but it was another to sleep on an empty beach.

Tessa took a few steps away from the water. She was wishing for one thing as she did that: not to be forced to have a conversation with Dean right now. He had aroused her curiosity and at the same time made her feel victorious. She had finally found a pleasant person who seemed reasonably normal, at least so far. But it wasn't just the conversation itself. The encounter had awakened a deeper interest inside her.

“Tessa!” he raised his voice to make sure the message reached the owner of the name.

She stepped onto the sandy path, not looking back.

“Are you going out with me tonight?” Dean continued, anticipating a positive response.

Tessa suppressed a smile. Wasn't that exactly what she wanted? Bingo!

“Where would you like us to go?” she asked, turning to look at him one last time before leaving.

“Come meet me in the hotel courtyard by the pool. Eight o'clock. I'll take care of the rest.”

Tessa smiled and made her way back to the hotel. A few seconds later, she realised that they hadn't even exchanged phone numbers. Just like decades ago. They would rely on pure trust. Romantic enough.

On a related note, Tessa's smartphone started ringing. It was Philip. Tessa frowned, but answered the call immediately. She owed him that, at least.

“Is everything okay?”

“Tessa! I heard you’re spending time on hot beaches. What's the weather like there? Are you having fun?”

“Very British of you. Yes, we have sun.”

“Good, good. I'm glad.” Philip muttered, rather dejected.

“But wait, how do you know where I am?”

“Oh. Well, let me explain. Ruby talked to your housemate.”

“Okay?”

“And he told us where to find you.”

“You would’ve found me on the phone anyway.” Tessa felt compelled to cram a little irony into the conversation.

“Anyway, Tessa!”

“Yes?”

“The reason I’m calling is that I have to break some news to you."

"Don't tell me you want me back in the office! Now that you know where I am, please don't do this to me!"

"It's an issue that concerns us all," he emphasised. "The department is being shut down."

Tessa stopped walking.

"What do you mean?"

"It's a problem we have been facing for some time. The higher managers have decided that your work can be shared between other departments. I'm sorry to let you down, but in two weeks' time we won't be a team anymore."

"Two weeks? I think it says a month in our employment contract!" she grew impatient, still trying to stay calm.

"I know. Changes have been made to a few paragraphs. I will detail it in an email."

"Did you know all this time?" Tessa asked, disappointed by her management's decision to drop the entire department.

"We tried our best to avoid the situation we are in now. Sorry. I made sure you got all your holidays sorted."

"To be paid less than if we had worked in the last few weeks. You know our holidays aren't fully paid." Tessa muttered to herself.

"Sorry, I didn't hear that."

"Nothing. " Tessa sighed. "Thanks for letting me know, Philip. I have nothing else to say."

"Tessa. I'm in the same pot. I lost my job too."

"Philip, you made more money than we all did."

Tessa was left with the phone in her hand and the damage in her arms. Tourists already in swimsuits ran by, carrying towels and fruit to the beach. The whole world around her seemed happy. The sky was cloudless and the sun was burning. Tessa looked up, bringing a hand to her eyes. The celestial sphere overwhelmed her. She suddenly felt as if the Universe was really listening. Maybe with just one ear. But the essence was there.

"What the hell?" she whispered, robbed of any other words.

CHAPTER SEVEN

“He didn't say shit! Not a single word! He called us all into the meeting room and dropped the bomb in front of us.” exclaimed Ruby on the video call.

“Excluding myself, I was on vacation.” Rebecca intervened. “I mean, I still am. I knew there was something rotten going on there.”

“And what do we do now?” Tessa spoke, sitting next to the mirror in her hotel room.

“We’re desperate. We can hide in a corner and scream.” muttered Rebecca.

“Is that sand in your hair?”

Tessa examined herself.

“You didn't say you're about to go to a warm country!” Ruby continued. “A free holiday…”

“I would’ve told you sooner or later,” Tessa replied, trying to get back to the main topic. “And the ‘warm country’ you’re talking about —”

“Sure! You were in such a rush to let us know that you turned your phone off without reading any of our messages.”

“Sorry.” Tessa apologised.

“She eats and sleeps for free and doesn't even send a picture to the poor people at home. It's cold here! It wouldn't hurt to see a photo where at least one of us is having fun.” Ruby continued.

“Okay. I think you’ve made your point, Ruby.” Rebecca picked up the conversation “Let's get back to what hurts the most.”

“I don’t know what to say. I’m confused.” Tessa replied.

“So were we yesterday when we found out.” Rebecca sighed. “But come on, at least good news for me: I don't have to put up with that creature any longer!”

“Fiona has definitely already found another job, leave her alone.” Ruby rolled her eyes.

“How do you know?”

“Native speaker — That’s what I know.”

“Come on, Ruby, that can be a downside sometimes. It's the only language she speaks.”

“Can you stop gossiping about it for a moment and focus on what's important?” Tessa hissed through her teeth.

“I think we all need to calm down and let things cool off.” Rebecca said, forcing a more mature tone than she had planned.

Tessa nodded.

“You haven't told us yet. So how's the city?” Ruby asked.

“It’s okay.” Tessa replied, slightly restrained.

“Come on, tell us more!” Ruby urged her, sticking her fingers together in Italian style.

“I'm going on a date tonight.” Tessa smiled and excitement could immediately be seen in her eyes.

“Oooh!” they both cheered in unison.

Tessa grinned.

“Details.”

“Uhm. He's American.” Tessa began to speak before she was interrupted by Ruby.

“Oh, Green Card! We’re on the right track!”

“Don't be silly, Ruby.”

“Tessa, I'm realistic. It's now, or never!”

“But I don't *need* a Green Card!”

“Everyone needs a Green Card.”

“Okay, I'll give it to you then.”

“If only…” Ruby sighed. “But it's fine, I'm going on dates too!”

“So is it over with Arif for good?” Tessa tried to clarify.

“Oh, yes. To hell with him! I’ve told you before that I don't want to see him again.”

“It's been a while and you haven't said a word. I just wanted to know where we’re standing. Joining me on the apps?”

“Nah… This kind of stuff isn't for me. I'm more about hooking up in person. You know, you go to a pub. You sit at a table. Alone. You smile at the guys that you find attractive. You see who kindly returns your smile… Methods like these. Old-school stuff, you know."

"Ruby, the way you present this idea sounds wrong." Tessa noticed, staring cautiously.

"Nah. That's how it used to be, and look, a lot of babies were born."

"Both of you, listen up!" Rebecca intervened. "Ruby, keep quiet. Tessa, give us more details about that American."

Tessa took a deep breath.

"I don't have much to say. He's talkative, but he doesn't talk too much. He's polite. Well dressed."

"It's a good start." Rebecca replied.

"What have I missed?!" Maggie exclaimed, joining the call as her children were crying in the background.

"Nothing much. We've lost our jobs and that's about it." muttered Rebecca.

"No, no! I already knew that. What's new with you guys?" Maggie added, trying to stay calm amidst the tumultuous chaos at home.

"Well, Tessa is on vacation on vouchers and she didn't say a word. We had to find out on our own." Ruby spoke, waiting for Tessa to feel guilty.

"Oh, that sounds amazing!" Maggie rejoiced. "No, baby, you're not allowed there!" she snapped for a second, then returned to the call. "Where exactly, Tessa?"

"Them warm countries!" Ruby emphasised.

"Leave her alone!" Rebecca sighed, rolling her eyes.

"I've got to go now. I think I'll start applying for new jobs today."

"Relax, Tessa! Just for the day. Worry about it tomorrow." Rebecca sighed, but the uneasiness she herself felt could be read on her face.

"I feel a little awkward when I think that I don't have a job to go back to." chimed Maggie.

"It's not as if you've really planned to come back, no?" Ruby tossed away a slightly stinging remark.

“You're not wrong there.”

“I’ll head off now.” Tessa greeted them.

“Ask him about his citizenship tonight!” Ruby exclaimed.

“Talk to you guys tomorrow!” Tessa struggled to hang up the call before it escalated again.

•

Darkness hadn’t quite fallen on the hotel courtyard yet, but corner lamps had begun to light up one by one. The pool water reflected on the hotel wall in undulating motions. Tessa wore a casual summer dress that wouldn’t look out of place at a formal event. She didn't know where Dean was going to take her, but she tried to look as nice as possible for any kind of situation. A soothing jazz echoed from the speakers strategically placed around the tables. Given the hotel pricing, Tessa was expecting live music. But anyway, what did she care? She knew she had a voucher in her purse.

Dean seemed to be running late. Looking at her watch, Tessa realised it was fifteen minutes past their meeting time. An old man who could be Tessa’s father and grandfather all together approached her. He seemed friendly and it could be seen from a distance that he was talkative.

“Are you waiting for someone?” he asked, realising she wasn't a local.

“That’s right.”

“He’s late, isn't he?”

“That’s right.”

“My date is late as well, but she's my wife.”

Tessa didn't know what to say, so she just squeezed a polite smile.

“Women, that's how they are." he added, shrugging, seeming to be pleased with his situation. “Are you also dating a woman?”

“I’m not. I also can’t say I can relate to what you’ve just said, but I do understand.”

"So it looks like there's a young gentleman in your life?"

"Not really."

"Have you been through a deep emotional devastation recently?"

The dialogue with the old man escalated way too quickly, Tessa thought. Who was he, anyway? And why did every word of his sound like an anecdote?

"Not really."

"I got married at the age of twenty-three. I'm not putting pressure on you, I'm just telling you. In our days, we only slept with our girlfriends after the wedding."

"That's why you got married at twenty-three."

"You hit the hammer on the head!" he said, noticing that his wife had come out of the toilet. "Look, there she is!"

Frowning, the old woman struggled to make her way towards him.

"You idiot, I've been looking for you everywhere!"

"Well, I got this far." he said to himself, finally tilting his head and saying goodbye to Tessa.

Tessa didn't have Dean's phone number. Not even his full name to look him up on social media. To ask if he was all right. She tried to find excuses - maybe he had been involved in an accident or she might have received the wrong address. Trying her best not to accept the truth - that he was late.

It was generally known the current generation was far too dependent on technology. People confirm ten times thirty minutes before a date, if it takes place or not. We plan through messages, because who calls these days? In the old days, our ancestors used to set a specific date and time for a gathering. Something like the last day of the last summer month of the year, half a year in advance. Both parties used to keep their commitment. In contemporary life, people can no longer rely on anything. Everything is relative. Yet, none of these stories excuse such behaviour.

Tessa of course didn't want to make false accusations towards Dean. Without consistent pretext, she didn't allow herself to judge him. Because here he was, pushing a borrowed bike. He was wearing a T-shirt and sports trousers. He carried a mountain backpack, flattened up so that it looked smaller. Dean wasn't too tall, but the long T-shirts he wore made him look shorter than he really was.

"Tessa!" he exclaimed, coming closer and stopping the wheel at her foot. "Have you been waiting for a long time?" he asked as an intro. It wasn't as if he really wanted an answer or to apologise for the delay.

"I've only just got here as well." she replied, smiling and pointedly not looking at the time. She was sure it was about twenty minutes past the set time already.

Nobody's perfect. An idea Tessa was trying to instill in her own code of conduct. She tried to be as patient as possible with her new acquaintances and she wanted to see the good in each of them. She had imagined that if she could detect a potential negative motive in someone, there were three other positive aspects inside them that were waiting to be discovered. And that's exactly what Tessa set out to do right away.

"Our reservation is in ten minutes. If we hurry, we arrive just in time. Just five minutes late."

"Okay, that doesn't sound too bad." Tessa smiled. "Where are we going?"

"To eat. You're hungry, aren't you?"

She didn't get a chance to approve or disapprove, as Dean was already continuing.

"I need to find a place to leave my bike first. I've been walking around for a century, but there's nothing here. I guess there should be something on the way."

"Do you live close by? Was it easier for you to cycle?"

"No, I'm forty minutes from here." he said, pointing at the path in which he was planning to go and Tessa followed. "But I ride bikes whenever I'm in a new city. That way I can experience the local energy. Get the vibes. Feel the local wind blowing onto my face. And I can memorise streets by actually cycling through them. It's much more interactive than being stuck on a bus."

There's some truth there, Tessa thought. Here's the excuse for being late. She was glad that she didn't judge him without thinking and that she had given him enough air to unfold and explain himself.

Unable to find a docking station for his bike, Dean leaned it against the wall next to the Italian place where he'd reserved a table for two.

The waiter pointed to the end of the room. Italians dined happily at the tables by the window and the fact that they were in a good mood was already a good sign.

"I heard good things about this place," Dean said, sitting on the couch against the wall, tossing his backpack beside him. "And I love Italian. I hope you do too! I'm sorry I didn't ask you before booking."

"Your choice is perfect," Tessa replied, taking a seat. "Thanks for the invitation."

"Anytime. I'm glad to finally find a real person in this city."

"A real person?"

"Yeah, you know. A creature with their feet on the ground. Someone who can have a decent conversation and who doesn't make me roll my eyes whenever they talk. Or someone who makes me run away before I even get to go for a walk with them."

"I can gladly sympathise."

"Already another point that we can add to the list of things that we have in common."

"What were the other points?" Tessa asked, curiously.

Dean smiled without saying any other word and lifted his menu, dipping his nose into the various pizza options. Tessa turned her menu from one side to the other, unsure of what she was craving. She didn't seem hungry, even though she hadn't eaten anything since lunch.

"What will you have?" she asked, not giving too much importance to the options she had displayed in front of her. What she wanted most now was to have a conversation.

"The appetisers look interesting, but don't waste your time with them."

"Affirmative."

"Do you like cheese?"

"I love cheese!"

"Ah, I should've figured. Women and cheese!"

"What's wrong with us?"

"Nothing. Do you like lasagna?"

"Yes. As long as it has cheese, there's no question."

"I like lasagna with parmesan cheese. It adds a salty aroma, almost like walnut."

"I see you know a thing or two about cheese!"

"Not even close! But that reminds me of a date I had a long time ago with a girl who said she loved cheese. I asked her about her favourite assortment. Answer: cheddar. And behold, people like that make me feel good about the minimal general knowledge I possess."

"I'm sure it's not exactly minimal."

Dean smiled again, not feeling the need to add a sequel to this topic.

"I think I'll choose a pizza," Tessa spoke, so as not to leave a gap in the conversation. "I'm not fussy."

"What do you mean by 'fussy'?"

"I don't make a big thing out of what I should have for food. I squeeze nutrients into myself to survive."

"Keep going…"

"I have nothing more to add. I don't enjoy eating."

"Then it means you're doing something wrong."

"What am I doing wrong?"

"I said *something* is wrong, I didn't say I knew what it was."

Tessa scratched the back of her neck.

"Okay. I'll eat pasta," he said. "How about we order a lasagna and share it?"

"Deal."

The kitchen, which was separated from the rest of the restaurant by a tiny wall, took their order right away. The waiter placed two glasses of water on the table. Dean claimed his share of plain water and urged Tessa to make a toast.

"It brings bad luck to do that with water!" Tessa insisted.

"Why?"

"Something about death. In addition, it's believed that it could bring rain." Tessa replied, raising her glass in spite of what she just said, to clink it with Dean's.

"Are you superstitious?"

"Not anymore."

A state of melancholy seized Tessa at the clink of their glasses. She looked at the front door, involuntarily waiting for rain to start falling. But it was hot outside, despite the late hour. Suddenly, a stranger lifted Dean's bicycle from next to the wall. He mounted it and pedaled away like lightning, all in almost a single motion.

Tessa turned her head to Dean. When he realised what was going on, he quickly stood up but it was too late to act.

"What did you just say about the rain option instead of bad luck?" he muttered, sitting back on his couch.

"Isn't it going to cost you money?!"

"Yeah, I'll take care of it later." he sighed, and then the waiter approached them with plates.

•

Tessa and Dean were digesting the food in peace. Or as relaxed as possible, because the next customers were keen to occupy their table next. In the end, the two relented and headed out. The streets were still brightly lit and lively.

"I got fired yesterday." Tessa spoke suddenly, feeling the need to shed words of sorrow.

"Fired?"

"Okay, maybe that's a strong word. My department's being shut down. That kind of leaves me jobless, in short." Tessa sighed, feeling a justified wave of worry taking hold of her again.

"That's life! Isn't it?" Dean replied at once, looking unmoved by her uneasiness. "Hey! I'm going on a family trip tomorrow! We'll be exploring the country for a week. Do you wanna join us?"

"Trip? Out of the blue?" Tessa tried to process what had just been thrown at her. She hadn't completely digested the previous topic, nor the pizza.

"Come on, it's going to be fun!"

Tessa shrugged, not knowing how to react. But Dean's sincere smile, and especially his straight, American, white teeth, firmly assured her that she was safe and had nothing to lose.

CHAPTER EIGHT

But money. Nothing to lose but money. Tessa dared to waste resources that her voucher-filled pocket didn't even have. Was this an immature decision? Absolutely! Would Tessa go ahead on the path she had chosen for herself? Certainly.

She gave the rest of her hotel stay to a homeless guy. He rushed to her bed as soon as he opened the door and marked his territory right there. Tessa was now the true gyspy. At least for next week… or so.

Dean's family was large, to her surprise. He had told her briefly about them before. But since Tessa had imagined Dean as a tourist, it was hard to associate him with a large group of relatives. It all somehow didn't click for Tessa. But here they were!

Irene. The little sister. A brunette with long straight hair arranged behind one ear. Her nails were clean and unpolished. Her phone case, however, was covered in silver and gold glitter. She was probably trying to fill the gap left by her plain manicure. Irene wore tights, a T-shirt, a hat and an air of nonchalance.

"A simple manicure denotes elegance." said Aya, noticing that Tessa had been staring at her daughter's fingernails for some time now.

Tessa hid her own hands behind her back, avoiding bringing her now half-polished nails into question. For in the wake of all that had happened, she had not had time to clean them. Unsure if the lady was referring to her, her daughter's nails, or if this remark was just an introductory greeting, Tessa chose silence. They hadn't exchanged a single line and Tessa was already feeling that the entire conversation was doomed to failure.

Aya was Dean's mother. Somewhere around the age of fifty, but she looked much younger. She wore a baseball cap. Half of it was missing due to fashion, which meant a good part of her head was left unshielded from the sun. She also wore tights. She could easily be mistaken as her daughter's sister. Her eyebrows were tattooed in a line that was perhaps a little too thin, but her skin was clean, shiny, and almost wrinkle-free.

"Of course." Tessa answered, late, almost useless now, for the pause between their remarks had become too long.

"I'm Senior!" the father introduced himself, kindly reaching out to shake Tessa's hand.

"Tessa." she smiled.

"I'm actually 'Dean Senior', but I prefer to be called 'Senior', and just that."

"That means…" Tessa added. "That you're Junior?" She looked at Dean.

"Nah, just 'Dean'."

"To each their own." Senior laughed.

Senior wore a grey newsboy cap. It matched his serene look and sporty outfit. He looked like he was advertising a detergent, given that he was completely dressed in white, less the accessory on the top of his head. He and the rest of the family seemed to be dressed for a round of golf. Tessa, on the other hand, looked like an outsider. Her assumption was confirmed when Kei, the older brother, appeared with an entire golf arsenal on his back.

"Hey! What's going on with the long faces? It's like you guys are at a funeral or something." he exclaimed, dragging his feet across the dry grass.

Kei was Dean's older brother. But with the way he threw the golf clubs to the floor and inhaled heavily, you'd be forgiven for guessing otherwise.

"Bro, I'm already tired," he complained. He appeared to change his mind immediately when he noticed Tessa. "Who is she? Your chick?"

Without hesitation, Dean grabbed Tessa by the arm, bringing her closer than necessary.

"Where are my manners!" he said, realising that they had all been quiet and eyeing each other awkwardly. “She's Tessa. I invited her to join us.”

True to their stereotypes, the American family immediately approved of the new acolyte and welcomed her to the team.

“Ready? Are we going?” Kei got excited.

“I don't think so.” said Tessa, looking down at her comfy but inappropriate outfit, when compared to the rest of the group.

“Don't worry, I'll take care of it.” Dean said in a low voice as if defending her from the rest of his family.

Golf wasn’t exactly Tessa's strong point. More precisely, she had never tried this Olympic sport before. So technically, she couldn’t give an opinion about her abilities yet. But the anxiety persisted.

The family was ambled across the freshly tended lawn, which appeared empty otherwise. Tessa waited at the entrance due to a lack of club-approved shoes. Dean appeared running, an arm full of clothes and a pair of shoes hanging from his little finger through the plastic ring of the label.

“These should be your size." he said, throwing the pile of clothes into her arms to get rid of their weight.

These were purchased from the club’s store, meaning they likely cost an exorbitant amount. Tessa had the impression that she had woken up in one of those books in which the modest main character meets a rich man who falls in love with her, offering her the whole world only in honour of unconditional love. The issue was that the story had not even developed visibly along the narrative thread yet. Tessa tried to give the clothes back, but Dean refused.

“You don't have to do this for me,” she said. “We barely know each other and I'm an independent woman. If I had the financial means to buy all of these right now, I would do. But because I'm not in this position, I refrain from it. Even the very idea that I agreed to venture into such a place in a foreign country is out of my budget.”

“You can return these when we leave.” said Dean, pointing at the cashier desk from which he had procured the equipment.

“Oh.” Tessa noted.

“We’re waiting for you, hurry up.” Dean added after giving her a nudge and before sprinting to the rest of his family.

Tessa glanced at the cashier, who raised her eyebrows.

"What are you looking at?" Tessa hissed to herself, trying not to actually be heard. "Do you have changing rooms here?"

She joined the group a few minutes later, armed with the right equipment. Irene offered a friendly smile.

"I've never played golf before." Tessa said to Dean.

"Don't worry. You have nothing to lose."

"Okay folks, let's get started," exclaimed Kei. "The team with the lowest score pays for dinner!"

Tessa looked desperately at Dean, who shrugged playfully.

"Mum will team up with Irene." Kei continued in the background.

"I was serious about saying I didn't play golf before." Tessa whispered to Dean.

"Relax, you can't lose against my Dad. He's the worst player I've ever seen."

"Dean and I." Kei continued. "And Dad will team up with…er…"

"Her name is Tessa." Dean added, proudly bringing her closer.

She looked at Dean again who gave her a sheepish smile, guilty because he had nothing more to say.

"Tessa." Kei concluded. "Okay, let's get to work!"

Aya and Irene advanced first, like two fierce fighters. Kei urged Dean to follow them.

"It'll be fine, good luck!" Dean encouraged her as she walked by.

Panic was visible on Tessa's face.

"Little rascals!" Senior muttered, putting his hands on his hips. "They brought us here to pay for their dinner. We'll show them!" he said, raising his chin. "Let's go, Tessa."

•

In London, Ruby sat down in a cool office chair and greeted the managers in front of her with a smile. The two of them were wearing three-piece suits, which intimidated Ruby in her favourite-yet-outworn jacket.

“Welcome, Ruby. We're glad to have you here.” said one of them.

Ruby looked at the certificates and awards on the walls and at the files that were neatly arranged on the shelves.

“We were impressed by your resume, so we'd like to hear more about you.”

"I'm Ruby," she said awkwardly as if this information wasn't already available to the employers. “Uhm, I’ve got ten years of experience in call centres and reservations in general. I’m punctual. I have a ‘can do’ attitude and the calm needed for such a job.”

“Of course. What made you apply for *this* position?”

Ruby looked through the polished glass that replaced one of the walls and noticed the employees. They sat at their computers in tailor-made suits with an exemplary posture, typing in a synchronous rhythm that already gave her anxiety. Ruby felt uneasy and afraid of the unknown. She knew very well that she had nowhere to go, for the former office no longer existed. Still, she knew she hated that job and would give anything to leave. Now that she was at that point, a longing gripped her.

“No problem.” said one of the managers when he saw that Ruby had fallen into thought and stopped focusing on their discussion. “Let me tell you more about us. Here we work in shifts. The first shift starts at six a.m. and the last one ends at ten p.m. From Monday to Sunday with two days off. You could work seven days in a row. We impose attire. For women, jackets, straight trousers and no shorter than knee-length skirts are welcomed. Only one pair of earrings is permitted and they should be gold, pearl, zirconia, or diamond if the situation allows. Any visible tattoos should be covered. We allow natural hair colours. Nothing flashy like green, purple or other inappropriate colours. Lunch break takes thirty minutes. During this time, the use of a mobile phone is permitted only in the kitchen or outside the building. During working hours, mobile phones are locked away in the hallway. Don't worry, you'll get your own key. We offer coffee cups and plastic water bottles inscribed with our company logo. We don’t allow these to be taken home, nor do we allow private items to be brought into the office. We do not allocate permanent desks to employees, the desks are occupied on rotation. Therefore, at the end of each shift, each employee gathers his folder with notes and places it in the closet.

Ruby tried to turn her attention back to the two managers, but her gaze got lost.

"Is everything all right, Ruby?"

"Yes. Yes, everything's okay. Sorry."

"Let's try another question then, Ruby. Where do you see yourself in five years?"

The telephones rang in the adjoining office, but the sound was inaudible, for the space was well insulated. The silence was oppressive.

"I'm sorry. I can't do this." Ruby replied, drawing the attention of both managers. "I can't see myself working here or in any other call centre in five years' time. Not even in a month's time! I can't do this anymore. I hate being such a slave and I hate myself because I've never tried anything else. It's all I know how to do. At my age, I should be able to do much more than a hungry student job."

The two managers looked at each other, not knowing how to intervene. Ruby stood up.

"The only reason I now know that I loved my former job is my colleagues. Sometimes they can be annoying, especially the English woman, but they're still my colleagues. I already miss the long mornings of gossip in the kitchen instead of working. I miss the quick breakfasts we had above our keyboard, because yes, we were allowed to eat at our desks. I already miss the days when half of my team were late for work and I miss making fun of those damn customers together with them. Because yes, some of them came from hell! I will miss the busy mornings at St. Paul's and the road to the office, among hurried citizens and umbrellas. I will miss the Fridays when we logged ourselves out and closed the lines earlier, just to escape from there. I already miss all of it, but I can't do it anymore. Sorry. Such a career is like a relationship predestined to fail from the very beginning. Like an ex-boyfriend who reappears in your life, again and again, only to hurt you and then leave you." said Ruby, now in tears. "In five years, I see myself doing something that brings me real joy. I'm sorry but it's not this job. I'm sorry I wasted your time. And thank you. It was time for me to come to my senses."

●

Back on the golf course, Senior and Tessa were leading the match. Kei fell to his knees, disappointed and dumbfounded at how he was managing to lose in front of his father and a stranger.

"I can't believe it! We're playing by family rules that I invented. How can I be losing?"

"Maybe if you're nice, you can learn something from the two."

"No way! Dean, I'm here to win!"

Senior's phone started ringing.

"Excuse me guys, it's work," he said, leaving the club in his wife's hands. "I'll be back in a moment."

"Now's the right time! Get her!" exclaimed Irene, pointing at Tessa.

"Oh no! That's not fair!" Tessa exclaimed as Dean tried to distract her.

Tessa ran, holding the club tightly in her hand, at the thought of avoiding Dean, who was following her at speed.

"It's over for you!" he exclaimed, hugging her to hold her in place. "She doesn't know how to play golf, she says!"

"Beginner's luck!" Tessa laughed, struggling for freedom until they both fell onto the grass.

"Where did these two meet?" Kei asked Irene in the distance. "I'm cringing."

"I've no idea." she shrugged.

●

It was evening and *Westfield* in Shepherd's Bush was getting more and more crowded with each passing second. Ruby sat down on the couch with a beer in each hand and began to sip eagerly. She was upset that she hadn't taken any action before. In a few months' time, she would be thirty years old. She felt like she had failed in every way. Even if she kept repeating to herself that she had no reason not to be proud of herself. She simply couldn't find the will to do so.

Emptying her second mug of beer, Ruby wiped the tears from her cheeks and checked her make-up in the small mirror in her purse. She rested her arm on the back of the couch and lifted her chin, trying to instill a little self-confidence. She smiled at a first passer-by, but he ignored her. She asked the waitress to bring her another pint.

Ruby dropped her fifth mug on the table and hiccuped, almost asleep. A young man sitting next to her was looking for her attention.

“Are you okay?”

“I'm fine! I'm fine.” she muttered, slapping her cheeks a few times. “I'll put my life in order. I'm going to be a new Ruby. A Ruby the world has never seen before. I don't know how I'm going to do that, but I'm going to get there.” she shouted, making the guy next to her get up and look for another table.

She sipped every last drop of beer and placed the empty mug with her growing collection. She could feel her head heavy and her surroundings spinning. Ruby let go of the beer handle and her head hit the table.

A car parked in front of her apartment. Ruby was asleep, her head propped against the window.

“We’re here. I think.”

These words made her wake up. She looked at the driver, who was not Arif, and whom she didn’t recognise.

“Who are you?!” She fumbled for the door handle and opened the door to be safe.

“I think you should take it easier with your drinking habits.” said the young guy, who bore a certain resemblance to Arif, but who was far from being him. “You almost fell down the stairs a few times on the way to the tube station. I realised I couldn't leave you alone.”

“Do we know each other?!”

“I don’t think we know each other. But you smiled provocatively at me from that couch of yours, hidden behind empty mugs of beer. I thought you'd probably smile at the next guy who passed you by and no one could guarantee that he'd be a good guy like me.”

“How do you know where I live?!”

“You told me. Insistently and repeatedly. I hope we're at the right place.”

Ruby examined the surroundings and the deserted street.

“Yeah… it’s the right address. Well, thank you.” she muttered, still nauseous.

She got out of the car, staggering to the entrance. The young man smiled good night and left right away. Still holding the keys in her hand, Ruby leaned against her doorway. She turned back to look for his car, but it had already turned towards the main street.

●

"Okay, okay! I know I promised not to answer my phone during the holidays, but what you're doing here is not fair!" exclaimed Senior, returning to the golf course.

Dean tried to distract Tessa from hitting the cup, while Kei struggled to make more points.

"Cheaters! I didn't raise cheaters!" Senior added, running with a raised finger towards Dean, who ran away, tossing Tessa's club to the floor.

"I'm hungry." Irene said to Aya, who nodded.

"Dinner, kids?" Aya asked, searching for everyone's attention.

"What's the score?!" Kei wondered, with the utmost childish sobriety.

"You lost." said Tessa.

"No, I didn't lose. You lost!"

Tessa shrugged.

"Children, children! I'm buying dinner tonight, don't worry." Senior waved his hands. "It was my fault I interrupted the game."

"Okay Dad, cool. I want BBQ."

"No, I want sashimi, Dad." Irene kicked her feet.

"I was thinking about fish as well." Senior approved.

"BBQ!"

"Sashimi, you fool!" Irene shouted.

"What would you choose?" Senior looked at Tessa, who just shrugged, glad she didn't have to pay out of her own pocket.

●

Ruby's doorbell rang insistently. A few knocks on the door. She was lying on the couch, still hungover, but the noise woke her up.

"Ruby, open the door, it's me."

She dragged her feet to the entrance, only to open up and see Arif in the doorway.

"What are you doing here?" she muttered, disturbed by the light of the lamp outside. "And actually, what are you ringing for? You've got keys."

"I know," he agreed, lifting the set of keys in front of her. "But it's your flat. I didn't want to burst in."

"Well, theoretically it belongs to three other people. Wherever they are. I haven't seen them in a decade."

"Right! Even more so then. Are you alright?"

"Okay, wait, why am I having a conversation with you right now?"

"Ruby, I'm here to apologise. I was stupid."

"Yes. I agree."

"I have nothing more to say to you than that I promise to respect and love you as you deserve."

Ruby still hesitated, but looking into his round black eyes, her knees felt weak again.

"Can I come in?"

She sighed, counting to three, then opened the door wide to make room for him.

●

The team stopped off in an indoor camping space, where various families rented a private space to relax. Children were playing around a pool of water that simulated a fishing pond. Several fathers were already trying their luck at catching fake fish. Ambient lanterns hung above the spacious tents, in front of which several couples dined. The ceiling simulated a starry sky dotted with stars, spread throughout the room. From time to time, a shooting star could be seen. Tessa stood motionless for a moment, staring at the artificial glittering and charming sky.

"I don't want this one. It smells like cat shit." Irene complained, waiting for another menu option from the bag Senior was sharing.

"Irene." Aya warned her.

"Sorry, Mum."

"Hot pot?" Dean asked Tessa and she gladly agreed.

Dean picked up a bowl of instant hot pot from his father's bag and patted him on the shoulder.

"Thanks, Dad, see you later."

While the other two siblings were still arguing over their favourite meals, Dean called Tessa over and gestured to the pool.

Dean unwrapped the package and poured hot water using the instructions. The two sat at the edge of the pool, isolated from the hustle and bustle of all the other families. The lights of the stars changed from time to time.

"These bags should make the water boil," Dean said, preoccupied with completing his cooking mission. "Tomorrow morning we leave for Cala Llonga. Have you been before?"

"This is my first time here."

"So you didn't go that way yet."

"I only visited the perimeter around my hotel, if that's what you want to ask."

"You don't really know how to enjoy a vacation, huh?"

"Look. I'm glad I got here."

"Agreed!"

Tessa smiled.

"You have a week left, don't you?" he spoke, gingerly taste testing whether the food was cooked or not.

"More or less. Less, actually. But, yes."

"Okay, let's do our best in these few days. What would you most like to achieve?"

"I'd like to go back to London and get a job. You know, a job worth waking up for in the morning. A company that would bring me real joy. And I miss the streets over there." Tessa smiled. "Buses and rainy streets. Overwhelming lights and people, always in a rush. I usually feel suffocating heat coming from the underground... enough to make me take off my scarf and jacket."

Dean was watching her intently, tugging on the T-shirt he was wearing as he also felt the warmth.

"I sit in the chair next to the exit and lean my head on the glass shield, which is a bit dirty and slightly scratched. A few commuters are leaning against it, but it doesn't bother me, because it doesn't affect me."

Dean stirs into the hot pot, listening intently. Now Tessa's eyes were closed.

"Someone is standing right in front of me, holding the bar above my head with one hand, holding a book in the other. His coat reaches to his knees and he staggers every time the tube slows down. Every time the tube starts moving, the panels along the stations become blurry, steamy, until they disappear from my sight and darkness takes their place. But not long after, it's replaced by another station, another lit platform, where loads of other passengers crowd towards the door. Some manage to get in, others have to wait for the next tube. It's almost a battle. I'm glad I managed to get a seat. I'm stepping out. I bring my card closer to the ticket machine. The little barriers open. I walk out of the underground and I feel the cool air caressing my cheeks."

"Interesting perspective." Dean approved.

"I get home, but I live somewhere else. Somewhere where no landlord bothers my sleep by chasing foxes."

"Foxes?"

"I live somewhere quiet. I'm sorry for Imo, but maybe I can take him with me."

"Imo?"

"Yeah, poor thing, he's broke too."

Confused, Dean continued stirring.

"Deep. I like the way you think. Thank you for sharing these images with me."

Tessa smiled, appreciating that she could have this conversation with Dean.

"Instead, I actually wanted to ask what your plans here in Spain are. As long as you've still got the freedom to choose."

"Oh." Tessa noted.

The northern lights were suddenly seen in the sky. Changing colours, accompanied by some applause from visitors.

"I think we can eat now," Dean handed Tessa chopsticks and a bowl. "Be careful, it's hot."

Tessa tasted the fragrant soup and immediately regretted biting into a vegetable she managed to fish out of the bowl.

"It's spicy." she said, struggling to chew at the same time.

"Pretty spicy, yeah."

Hungry, Tessa tried a piece of meat which she chewed carefully.

"Kind of artificial."

"Yeah," Dean agreed, sipping noodles, vegetables and meat from the same mouthful. "I don't know where he bought these from."

Tessa shrugged and she continued to eat, despite the synthetic taste.

"I've been to London a few times. I like it there."

"On what occasion?"

"My mum had some work to do there and I went with her. I also lived in France for a few years. I like Europe. I think people have more charm over here than in the States."

"You think so?

"Absolutely. Here you are at the source. The same goes for Asia. Africa. You know what I mean."

"I guess. I think so." Tessa replied, in tears, because she couldn't stand the sharp taste anymore.

"Are you okay?"

"I don't know." she replied, winding up and trying to cool off.

"Here you go." he handed her a bottle of water. "Do you still want the rest?"

Tessa shook her head. Dean took a sip of the remaining soup and his face went red. Meanwhile…

"This isn't water!" Tessa shouted, immediately putting down the bottle that instantly burned her throat and stomach.

"Whoops. It's whiskey." Dean agreed, expecting a reaction from her and hoping she wouldn't be upset.

Tessa took another sip, this time ready for what was to come.

"Why do you have whiskey with you?" she asked.

"Why not?" he took the bottle from her hand to have a sip. "Want more?"

"Why not?" she said, taking the bottle back, wiping the sweat off her forehead. "I think I intoxicated my taste buds with these preservatives."

"I know what you're saying. Get some whiskey. Wash it off."

"That's what I'm doing."

Dean laughed, sitting comfortably next to Tessa. He then stroked her hand and went in for a hug.

"The wildest fantasy I have right now is for you to fall asleep on my arm." he whispered.

Tessa expected the sky to turn into a wonderful show, a story, a dream, with shooting stars and twinkles from afar. But this didn't happen. No stars fell. Instead, Dean hugged her tightly, replacing a thousand shooting stars with his gesture.

CHAPTER NINE

Arif got dressed and rushed out the door, but not before giving Ruby a forehead kiss.

"See you soon!" he shouted from the sidewalk, still clad in the office jacket he had arrived in the night before.

Ruby tried to smile, despite the unpleasant sensation lurking in her stomach. It was as if all the choices she had made lately were ominous. But most likely it was just a hangover.

Wearing her pyjamas, she arrived at the corner shop. She helped herself with a bottle of milk from the fridge and some ramen from the discount corner. Lined up at the cashier's desk, she turned the key on her finger, trying to stay awake, at least until she left the store.

"Oh, hey! You again." said a voice at once, causing her to turn and look at the fruit section.

"You." she recognised the stranger who drove her home just a few hours ago.

"Are you feeling better today?" he asked, stepping in the queue behind her.

"I'm okay."

He approved with a smile.

"But what are you doing here?!" she hurried to ask.

"I moved here recently."

"Here?! Why would you live in this area?"

"Why do you live here?"

"I'm broke." she muttered, rolling her eyes with attitude. She immediately regretted the gesture and what had been said earlier, noticing that she was behaving strangely, just to bring an air of importance to the conversation.

"Well, I didn't mean to upset you or give you the wrong impression yesterday. But I was worried you wouldn't get back safely. You shouldn't drink that much."

"Next customer, please." cried the cashier.

"My name is Ruby." she then said, turning her full attention to him.

"I'm Raresh. Nice to meet you."

"Next!" the cashier insisted, having no patience for anything other than getting through the line of customers.

"Well, Ms. Ruby, I think you're needed." Raresh laughed, pointing with elegance towards the counter.

"Maybe we'll see each other around again."

Raresh smiled benevolently.

●

Tessa's phone had been ringing again and again for more than ten minutes. She woke up with a slight headache. She sat up and looked around like a child, trying to remember where she was. Dean was sleeping soundly. Tessa wondered why she fell asleep in the weirdest places when she was with him.

His presence made her feel safe. That was the answer. Families and couples got out of tents scattered throughout the place. The remains of hot pot were thrown at Tessa's feet. She picked up her still-ringing phone, pressed it to her cheek, and laid on her back, shoulder to shoulder with Dean.

"Yes?"

"T!" Imo snapped, in a slightly hoarse voice as if he had eaten a whole box of ice cream while screaming at a football game in front of the TV. "We've messed up!"

"Huh?"

"This flat!"

"Do you mean the location or —"

"T, in my opinion, we're in trouble."

“I don't get it. What are you talking about?” she got up on her feet, hoping that this gesture would have a positive effect on her understanding.

“Farisita is evacuating us.”

“Wait. Why? When?”

“Starting tomorrow. That's how she wants it.”

“That’s not legal!” she got impatient, but in a whisper, so as not to make a big fuss in public.

“You know we don't have a proper contract. I think I'll sleep with my sister for a few nights.”

Tessa felt like a boulder was being bound to her foot, pulling her down to the bottom of the ocean.

“I think you'd better come home, T. I'm sorry.”

She sighed, agreeing, knowing she had to face her responsibilities as a tenant and even more so as a housemate and friend.

Yet here he was, Dean, sleeping like an angel on the floor by her feet. Suddenly, the ocean no longer seemed as deep, but instead turned into a surface of solid earth, covered by fragile and fragrant grass.

“I can’t.” she replied, knowing that she had made one of those selfish and dramatic decisions.

“You can’t?”

“Imo, I already owe you to heaven and back.” She took a deep breath. “And I have one last request. Please throw all of my things into a suitcase and keep them with you until I’m back.”

“Okay, T. But know that no matter how much I want to support you, there's no room for two more people in my sister's flat.”

“Just the suitcase, please. A few days until I get back.”

“Cool.”

“I owe you one, Imo!”

“It's okay. But what do you have in mind?”

“I'll be fine.” Tessa smiled, confident that she knew what she was doing.

●

Cala Llonga. Or rather, the last stop and the end of Tessa's trip.

"Cute. You're cute!" a parrot's voice roared at her.

"Uhm. You're cute too." Tessa replied.

Dean had appeared with a grey parrot sitting comfortably on his shoulder. Cars drove behind the two, but the bird was motionless and accustomed to the idea of being in public. Tessa had a lot of questions on her mind that were burning to be queried aloud. Prominently, there was the lack of a job when returning to London. The fact that she was technically homeless until she found a new place to live. What was going to happen to the connection between her and Dean? And where did this parrot come from? What is going on?!

"It's an African Grey." Dean spoke, scratching the top of the bird's head. It shivered.

"You're cute," it squawked.

"You're cute too, Freddie."

Tessa looked at them both without making a sound.

"Freddie is a family member too and we make sure he has everything he needs when we're not with him. He's usually waiting for us here." Dean pointed to a flat above a grocery store behind Tessa. "He feels good in his home and the caretaker makes sure he's spoiled. Isn't that right, Freddie?"

"You're cute," Freddie replied.

"I think we still have to work on enriching his vocabulary, but at least he hasn't learn how to swear. Yet." Dean was amused. "But yeah, I thought you might want to say hello."

"Hi, Freddie." Tessa tried to befriend him.

"You're cute."

"I agree," said Dean. "She's pretty, isn't she? I think her nose is especially nice. It seems to have a personality of its own."

Freddie made an approving sound, which made Tessa laugh.

"And I think you're in the top one list of the sexiest men alive." Tessa affirmed.

"Who? Freddie or me?"

"You!"

"And who's second place?"

"There's no second place."

"Wait. Who else is on this list?"

"Only you."

“Hm. Then I don't think I feel as flattered without competition.”

“Hm.” Tessa thought about what she just said.

“Cute. You're cute.” Freddie concluded.

Then Dean hugged Tessa. Without warning, without her anticipating his move. Freddie nestled next to the two.

“What do you think about me?” Dean asked in one breath.

“What *I* think about you?”

“Don't repeat my question, just answer me.”

The sun was beating down, but Tessa's desire to not let go of him was even more intense.

“When one’s heart beats too hard to hear any thoughts, I think the lack of words says it all.”

Hearing this, Dean breathed a sigh of relief.

“I like you too, Tessa.” he added, now trying to look her in the eye.

“But what do we do? This Tessa lives on the other side of the world and is madly interested in being yours.”

“Do you like me that much?”

“Inexplicable and undeniably. Whatever the reason, it seems like I do. How unfortunate.”

Or maybe Tessa just felt deserted. Dean's closeness reassured her that life was exciting. The idea of losing him would have thrown her straight to the beginning of the story. And because thoughts always became reality, a presentiment was already nestled in this scenario.

“I'm leaving tomorrow morning.” Tessa hurried to say.

“I'm going back to the States.” Dean also wanted to throw news at her, as if he didn't want to be left out when it came to making announcements. “After the end of this year, I'll probably take a break for a year or two.”

“I urgently need a job. And a place to stay. I think bad news is all coming at once.”

“I'm trying to develop this app I'm working on. Who knows, maybe there's something good coming out of it. I'll be in Florida, most likely. I need sun to be creative.” Dean continued, as if taking part in a competition to share personal issues.

Trying to sound sympathetic, Tessa nodded. A local walked out of the wooden home nearby. He brought with him a stack of magazines for the corner kiosk. A *Forbes* magazine fell at Tessa's feet. Dean didn't care, being too absorbed in the conversation. Or maybe his own ego.

"Tessa, I'm glad to know you exist and I think we'll definitely meet again someday."

There was this magazine and it was smiling at Tessa. With Irene and Senior on the cover.

"That's all?" she whispered, looking back at Dean, merging two topics into one question.

"I mean, you know, life isn't easy." he shrugged, and then Freddie shook his feathers. "I thought a lot about the two of us last night. I think you're great, and you certainly caught my attention. If we stay friends, we may be able to meet at some point when our paths intertwine again."

Disappointment was engraved on Tessa's face. But she deserved every bit of distress. For her expectations have brought her here. That was life.

"Sure. We can be friends." Tessa murmured, unsure of what kind of words her lips were touching.

"I hope you find someone nice, you deserve it. You need someone to make your life more colourful. Unfortunately, I don't think it can be me. Sorry, Tessa."

"Why do I feel like we're in the middle of a breakup?" She tried to hide her tears with a smile. "We weren't even together."

"You know, you really need someone to fit your lifestyle."

Gathering her courage in one breath, Tessa filled her lungs with bravery. The magazine stood motionless at her feet. Dean noticed it now.

"Do you think there's something wrong with my lifestyle?"

"I don't think there's anything wrong with the way you live, no. It's just that we're very different, that's all. And I also think you're agitated. A little too frantic for my taste. I'm looking for someone calmer."

Tessa approved, processing this information.

"You're cute!" Freddie shuffled.

"Dean, I'm sorry I can't afford a two-year vacation to focus on insight into my future. Throughout this whirlwind of life, I forget if there is or ever was any passion left in me. I have a stressful career that I hate. I had a job where people used to ring me to spell their names as 'O' from 'Osama bin Laden' and now I'm upset because

I've lost this job. A lot of things go wrong for me and you're right that we're not part of the same society. A rainy city and a life that needs to be put in order is waiting for me."

Freddie shook his feathers. Dean wanted to hug Tessa for the last time but instead decided to lift *Forbes* off the hot asphalt and place it under his armpit to quietly leaf through it later.

The ground beneath felt like it was growing between them, creating a vast gulf of emptiness. The sudden chill in the air made it clear that they belonged to two different societies in the same Universe.

●

Ruby pushed open the sliding door of the Canary Wharf office, still keeping her fingers crossed for the job interview she had just finished. She adjusted her skirt with both palms and looked up at the glass buildings. A vivid premonition flooded her chest, as if a fresh start was knocking on her door.

And right there, next to the tube station, was Arif. Hugging and kissing what appeared to be a co-worker. Ruby was standing a few steps away from them, like a cloud heavy with water being pushed by the wind at the beginning of a storm.

"You piece of shit!" she muttered, squeezing one of her shoes off and throwing it at him.

Arif noticed her presence and tried to apologise in the middle of the action. But Ruby took off her left shoe as well and threw it into him. Arif shook his head.

"Ruby, honey, stop."

He approached to calm her. But Ruby raised a finger, distancing herself from him. She still had some self respect left. Without another word, she rushed to the escalator. She remembered that she was barefoot, so she ran back, lifted her shoes, and disappeared. After what seemed to her to be the longest escalator ride in the city, Ruby got lost in the crowd and Arif faded from her story.

On a dark street somewhere in Hounslow, Ruby's shoes swayed in the darkness. Their belts hung between her fingers as she walked too close to the road. A car slowed down next to her, accompanying her for a while until the driver's window came down. Raresh tried to get her attention whilst keeping an eye on the road. Ruby was staring at the ground and nothing seemed to interest her enough to distract her. Raresh honked. Ruby winced and her shoes slipped out of her hand.

"Good evening, Ruby!" he raised his voice to make himself heard.

Ruby frowned, not knowing how to interpret his presence.

"I brought fried chicken and beer. Are you hungry?"

"How did you know?"

"That you're here or that you're hungry?"

"Both." She looked from left to right. "Stalker."

"I live here, remember? This street is the only one that takes me home."

"Oh." Ruby scratched her forehead. "Yeah, I don't know. I'm kinda dizzy."

"Okay. You don't get any beer in this case, but the chicken is yours."

An avalanche of horns from cars waiting to pick up speed was heard in the background. Ruby hurried and jumped into the car, allowing Raresh to speed up.

Parked on Primrose Hill, the two opened the box of fried chicken.

"Why did we drive this far? The food got cold."

"Sorry. It's my favourite place in London," he said. "I wanted to share this moment with you."

The illuminated city had a different charm observed through the car's windshield. Ruby propped her bare feet on the dashboard, helping herself with fried chicken. Somewhat puzzled, Raresh examined her gesture. But noticing Ruby's quiet smile, he took off his shoes as well and propped his feet up, imitating her gesture.

"Can I have your number?" he asked after a moment.

"Which number?" she stammered.

"Your number."

"1991." she answered promptly.

"Okay." he snorted with laughter. "I found out how old you are. I'm glad to know we're the same age."

Ruby blushed, but wasn't quite sure why.

"I actually wanted to have your phone number."

"Oh." she realised. "Sorry. I think I'm the one going through a premature mid-life crisis. Sure, you can have my phone number, too."

"Okay!" he rejoiced.

"Okay." she nodded approvingly, helping herself to some food.

Silence settled around the two, but the calm of the evening and the smell of fried chicken said more than enough.

CHAPTER TEN

Some people say that the friendzone is that dark place where you throw your soul mate, for fear that you'd hurt him with the truth. For fear that you'd cause him pain, if he knew you liked him more than just as a friend.

Travelling is weird. When you leave, you miss home. When you're back home, you feel sorry that the trip is over.

But Tessa couldn't agree with her own statements this time. Everything seemed upside down. She waited on the stairs to board the plane, crowded with the rest of the low-cost passengers. She let several people climb in front of her. They rubbed their shoulders onto hers, one by one, as if they were trying to assert dominance and punish her for standing in their way. Tessa felt she didn't belong. On the plane's stairs and in general. She wasn't sure if she was disappointed, sad, angry, everything together, or exasperated in general. She blamed herself for raising her expectations too high. Now that she had put all her hopes into Dean, she felt she had no other choice. It all ended with him.

Sitting in her seat, crowded on the left and the right by passengers, Tessa folded her arms and felt the need to hug someone. Tempted to cover her ears with her palms, she refrained. For she knew that these thoughts came from within.

•

"He cheated on me. With a chick with an ugly mustache." Ruby spoke, clenching her fists.

"Wait, I thought the whole story about Arif was over."

"That's right. I'm done. All right now."

"You go girl! But wait. Wait, wait, wait. You said you went out last night." exclaimed Rebecca.

"Yup. A new guy."

"I think I'm lost in the narrative."

The sun was shining through the clouds, but the wind was cold enough to make Rebecca zip up her jacket. The two were the only ones on that balcony, because the rest of the employees had, well, a job.

"What can I say! At least he brings food!" Rebecca added.

"I think he only cares about his car and the food." Ruby sighed muffledly.

"It seems to me that you don't know how to appreciate quality when you see it."

Ruby looked down at the traffic on the road and sighed again.

"I don't know. Maybe."

"Surely!"

"He asked for my phone number."

"See! Exactly what I was just saying. Keep him close. I think he's good quality."

"He actually asked me for *a* number. And I wasn't sure if it was my date of birth or my phone number. So I gave him both.

Rebecca grimaced in confusion, but then tapped her friend on the shoulder. She knew there was no way to change her, only to accept her as she was.

●

Tessa got off the bus at Marble Arch, pulling her suitcase up the footpath.

Double-decker buses. Rushed pedestrians. Cyclists riding with speakers and loud music attached to the bottom pipe of their bikes. They all reminded her that she was home again.

She stretched out her right arm, catching the first drops of rain in her palm. Immediately, she felt safe. In a cool corner of the world that was also somehow warm and welcoming. As miserable as she felt when she boarded that plane, the better her mood was once she stepped on familiar ground. Having a place to come back to, no matter what would've happened, was a gift Tessa didn't even know she had. Feeling at home in total chaos was a talent that she realised she possessed, only after a time away from the source.

The Central Line was stifling. Just as she had left it. Tessa brought sadistic enthusiasm with her as she descended the stairs. She was ready to sweat in the sauna that was so dear to her. Train headlights. Tessa was always careful to take at least one step back from everyone else on the platform. Just to avoid the possibility of being pushed on the rails by a neurotic.

The tube stopped at the station. Passengers pushed towards the doors before those standing inside even got off. Some changed their minds at the last second and switched direction. Others waited in seclusion on a bench. Briefcases and jackets got stuck between the automatic doors. Foreigners suddenly became allies, banding together to free the passengers in pain. Puppies were looking for their way to their owners' favourite door. Ladies were changing from heels to trainers.

Tessa imagined this scene in slow motion and all the puzzle pieces came together. Her renaissance painting came to life again, reminding her why she loved this city.

She moved from east to west, rushing to get home. From one escalator to another, trying not to catch her trainers between the escalators during this operation. Several residents soaked to the bone appeared and hurried towards the only escalator that was operating. One of them shook raindrops off of his umbrella.

That caught Tessa's attention.

The speeding tube blurred into an illusion. Tessa turned around, completely changing her mind.

It was getting dark at Leicester Square Station. It was always jarring when there appeared to be a time jump after emerging from the underground. Tessa made her way through the passers-by until she reached a corner of Chinatown. The storm was intensifying.

June Storm was just as she had left it.

“Have you seen Nev?” she asked Colin, who greeted her with a smile.

"He left a few minutes ago."

Tessa nodded and returned to the street, bringing her suitcase with her to the alley behind the bar. Luckily for her, Nev was still present and moving toward an old, damp wall. Tessa recognised him right away by the jacket he was wearing. By the haircut that gave him away. By his walk. By his presence that emanated confidence.

"Hey!" she shouted enthusiastically, expecting to be greeted with applause.

Then she realised that she had forgotten to even tell him about her trip. However, she was sure he had missed her. Just like — she had realised now — she had missed him.

"Hey!" she insisted and Nev stopped.

The neon lights lit up at the opposite restaurant. Rain and light prevented her from having a clear picture. And yet. Her fiery smile faded as Nev turned to face her.

"Where's your umbrella, milady?" he asked, blood running down his nostrils as the rain washed his face.

"I thought you brought one." she murmured, frozen, not knowing how to react.

"Not this time." Nev smiled, taking a step to the right.

He fell at once next to the wall as if inertia was trying to knock him down and hold him to the ground. Tessa's suitcase tipped into a puddle as Tessa ran towards him. Nev vomited white contents, which immediately mixed with the blood covering his chin. The spasms made him involuntarily hit his head against the wall. Tessa struggled to lift him up, but fell beside him, trying.

"What's wrong?!"

Tessa panicked. Didn't know what to do.

"What's going on?"

"Life."

Tessa searched inside her pocket.

"I've already called them."

She looked up, noticing the white powder covering his T-shirt underneath his jacket.

"You talk to me about stupid laws and rules, like you can have anything and you can be anyone." Tessa shook her head, grabbing him by the shoulder. "And you?! What did you do with that?

Nothing. It's some nonsense that doesn't exist."

"I'm the coach, milady. I don't play." he replied, and his sly smile faded when a violent spasm took its place.

"Nev...?"

But he could no longer hear her. Tessa tried to keep his eyes open, but his gaze appeared lost. The trembling forced him to spit blood. His sweat was washed away by the torrential rain. Tessa looked around for help, but the surroundings were deserted like never before. As if the street was hidden away from reality. Isolated from the world.

CHAPTER ELEVEN

"Cardiac arrest is just a step away from him. He was lucky this time. I recommend talking to a counselor tomorrow morning." said the doctor, heading for the next hospital room.

For a moment, Tessa stood in the narrow hallway of University College Hospital staring at the glossy floor. Her suitcase was propped up by the door. She finally had the courage to face her friend.

"Hey," she murmured, walking closer to the bed Nev was laying in, his face less pale. "How do you feel?"

"I'm alive, milady. As it should be." he said, giving out a tingling laugh, almost like a hiccup.

Several people in the room turned their attention to the two.

"I don't find this funny," said Tessa in a low voice.

"I think it is. That's life. Witty at times."

Tessa sat on the edge of the bed. Nev tapped her on the back of her hand.

"Thanks for saving my life."

"You called for help on your own."

"Yes, but an angel kept me company while I waited."

The people in the room pretended to not listen anymore.

"I don't think you're aware of what you're doing. This stuff is going to kill you one day."

"But that day is not today."

"I'm serious. What did you take this time?"

"Nothing."

“What was it?”

“Irrelevant. Completely irrelevant.”

Tessa sighed.

“Where is your family?”

“I have no family, milady.”

“Everyone has a family.”

“Not true.” Nev smiled and the gravity on his face now made Tessa realise she had made a mistake in making her own assumptions.

“Friends then?”

“We're not in some American movie, milady. I'm not important. No one will write a parallel plot for my character. That’s separate from the main narrative. Nobody cares about my past. My present is important.”

“Good thing you said it yourself. You're ruining your present now and here.”

“Sorry.” he murmured, more to get rid of her insistence.

“You need help.”

Nev smiled, flattered by Tessa's care. His watery eyes revealed the stubbornness that persisted in the fantasy world in which he lived and from which he didn’t plan to part.

“I can't lose you, Nev! My mood since I met you is *Bohemian Rhapsody*. It goes from one genre to another in just six minutes. And as bizarre as it sounds, it's brilliant. My life is a mess. And the more I ask for, the more I discover that I add fulfilled desires to this pile of feelings and events that excite me and confuse me at the same time. I was plain before I met you. I still am! But my life has turned into a mess that I want to remember decades later and laugh about.”

The other patients stared back in sync. Nev pulled the curtain that separated them from him.

“How can I know so little about you and still like you so much?”

“It's because you don't know me, milady. If you knew me better, you would see that there is nothing to adore about this person I am.”

“I disagree.”

“Since when?”

“From now on.”

“Oof. Sounds like trouble to me. I think we're in a dangerous zone.” Nev added, sitting comfortably by the pillow on the wall.

“A person lives only once. I think you’re wonderful and I might endlessly regret it if I don’t confess my feelings.”

“There is nothing to adore about me.” Nev shook his head, not wanting to accept these words.

“You always have to have an opinion on everything. Just let me like you. The further you push me, the tighter I will cling to you.”

“It is my right to have any opinion I want!” he raised his voice, slapping his chest. “I have a right to hate myself, you, and anyone else in this Universe.”

“You don't hate yourself, Nev. And I think you're nice. Even when you involuntarily shout at me.”

“Still, I'm not that great, milady.”

“You’re right. You're horrible!”

Tessa was waiting for a reaction. Immediately, his smile turned into a peal of sincere laughter. Tessa breathed a sigh of relief. At that moment, Nev took her hand and kissed the back of her palm. Tessa couldn’t hold back.

“You bumped into me one day. You didn't say much, you didn't do much, but I knew, I realise now, that I wanted to be around you for the rest of my life.”

“What did I do to you, milady?” he chuckled.

“You existed.”

“Other people do exist too.”

“But they’re not you.” Tessa smiled. “I'm home again and I’m *happy*. If I were to sum up all the madness and reduce it to one word. How I wish you were me, for at least a day! To see what I see and feel what I feel.”

“I know exactly what's going on, milady. It's not a coincidence. But I will have to disappoint you if you continue to deceive yourself. We're friends, right?”

“Friends.” Tessa agreed after long hesitation, reaching out to shake his hand.

And so, the friendship between the two was sealed.

“What's with that suitcase? Where have you been? Who broke your heart?”

“Holiday.”

“Oh, vacation!” he breathed out excitement.

"I lost my job."

"Oh."

"My flat. And a possible relationship."

"Wow — Wait a second! Can you repeat that? From the beginning? How many centuries have I lost, milady? Did I hit my head and fell into a coma?"

"Two weeks. It's a long story that drove me mad and I couldn't wait to tell you about it. But at this point it has all faded and it seems just a distant memory."

"I have time to listen to immortal stories. I'm not going anywhere." Nev laughed. "I mean, I wish I could, but I'm afraid to take these infusions out on my own." he whispered.

Tessa laughed and sat down comfortably beside him.

"I don't know where to start, but I think I know what I want now. I know who I am and I know what I'm looking for."

"It's good to think you know, milady. However, I think you're confused and I'm now doubting which one of us is the one who snorted too much cocaine."

"Okay, let me start from the beginning."

Some patients had already both ears ready for this one.

CHAPTER TWELVE

"I want you to come to a party with me." Nev spoke, rolling a cigarette between his fingers.

"You promised you were giving up on these." Tessa replied, snatching it from his hand.

"I beg you. It's a regular cigarette."

Reluctantly, Tessa returned it to him.

"What party?"

"It's a networking event. Actors, producers, musicians. Creatures of this type." he said, lounging on the bench in Hyde Park.

Although it was still summer, autumn had begun to creep in.

"Why would you take *me* there?! I'm not prepared to have a discussion with such people."

"Don't worry. The vast majority are rather a bunch of losers when it comes to their profession, milady. Huge egos, limited talent, manufactured careers. But my intention is different. They are somewhat open and talkative. They are what you covet."

"I'm not following."

"Milady, we live in a big world filled with opportunities and you haven't tasted the sweet ones yet."

"You'rc right. I licd."

"What are you talking about?"

"I said I knew what I wanted. I have no idea what I want."

"And that's exactly why I'm here. For a little guidance. Now allow me to set out my thoughts."

"I'm listening."

"I'm a man, aren't I?"

"Yes…?"

"Excellent. This is my industry. The territory in which I excel."

"What are you talking about?"

"I will reveal to you the greatest secret to a well-deserved and emancipated life."

Tessa was waiting for the next words.

"The secret to conquering ferocious males!" he exclaimed proudly.

"Oh, Nev… I think I've had enough. I don't want to hear about any more disastrous encounters. Even less about individuals who don't know what they want. Sometimes at night, before bed, I think about —"

"Okay, milady! He ghosted you. In the nicest way possible. It happened to us all before."

"Worse. He friendzoned me. Moreover, it made me realise that I'm the kind of person who's happy to receive vouchers and live off them. I've had enough. I won't waste my time with such attempts any more."

"Here is the heart of the matter. Milady needs to know what she wants, nothing else."

"I don't know what to say to you. It's not that easy. I lost my mind looking for the perfect relationship in what feels like a hopeless, relentless pursuit of dates. I wish everything was simpler." she said, kicking a pebble that rolled to the side of the road.

Nev looked for Tessa and just then she made a connection between her own words and those of her friend.

"What a soulless idiot you are!" exclaimed Tessa, as if a revelation was pouring out on her.

A few passers-by turned their eyes to them. Satisfied, Nev nodded. He let out a tickling laugh.

"My, my. Don't tell anyone you're discriminating."

"The solution is to behave like a man!"

"No, not really." he smiled. "The secret is to behave like a woman. But to feel like a male. Simple. An even more deadly combination than us men possess."

•

Ruby was still on a job hunt. When Tessa returned to London, she settled down on Ruby's couch until she could find another place to rent.

"I should seriously focus on applying for a new job." Tessa spoke, her mind fluttering in thousands of directions.

"How many positions have you applied for?" Nev asked, leafing through Tessa's wardrobe.

"Two hundred."

"That should be enough. Stop overthinking. I promise you that every trouble will settle down at the right time." he replied, unable to choose the right dress for Tessa.

"What do you represent today? The protagonist's gay best friend in a romantic comedy?"

"Dammit. On the contrary. I tried, but I can't give my opinion here. Choose your outfit, milady. I'm overworked."

Tessa picked up a silk dress without giving it too much importance. In the meantime, Nev filled two glasses with cold tap water.

"Perfect! It looks like we could go to an expensive restaurant and pretend we're rich! We'd then just have to sneak out before the bill arrives." he spoke as he arranged his tie in the mirror by the front door.

"Ah, give me a break… I don't want to hear any more." Tessa muttered, holding onto her dress.

"Come on, come here." he called her to the dining room table, where he had placed the two glasses of water.

"These are Ruby's new glasses!" Tessa shouted, only now seeing what Nev had been up to at the last minute. "She never uses them. She's gonna kill us!"

"Don't worry. I'll take the responsibility."

"She doesn't know you're here. She doesn't even know who you are!"

"Exactly."

"You're getting me in trouble."

"Milady, it's no big deal."

Tessa rushed into the bathroom and reappeared right away wearing her dress.

"Look who's ready to tackle life!" Nev exclaimed.

"I feel plain," said Tessa, looking down at the material of her dress. "Boring."

"You are as you should be. Wonderful."

"You're flattering me, but stop describing me as a superhero."

"I just described you as a woman who deserves a compliment. Heroism comes later."

Sighing, Tessa nodded but remained relatively unconvinced.

"Milady, here's what the problem looks like. You can't pour your wishes and future into a shattered glass. Chin up. I miss the young lady who, despite being subjected to unnecessary daily stress and who was most of the time completely disorganised, didn't lose the power to be confident. I think I'm starting to forget what it's like to deal with this side of my lady. If your heart doesn't want to wear a dress, wear trousers instead. If leaving home in your pajamas makes you happy, do so. If lipstick excites you, apply it. Us men can't notice it anyway. But most importantly, don't wait for a man to tell you all of this. And I'm very aware of the irony. I just wish I had my lady back. Disoriented, but strong. That's her!"

There was a pause. "I want to wear the dress."

"Then there we have it." Nev said simply. Tessa hurried over and hugged him tightly. "Before we leave, I want to do one more thing." he added, walking to the table where he had left his water glasses. He drank from one of them and placed it next to the full one. "Oof! I was thirsty."

Tessa waited for him to continue.

"So this is yours." he spoke, placing his full glass into her right palm. "I want you to ignore everything that ever hurt you. It's desirable to imagine your future, through the prism of an ideal present."

Closing her eyes, Tessa held the glass in both hands.

"I want you to feel the joy that this imaginary present brings you."

"You know what, Nev?" she whispered, looking at him. "I already feel free and relaxed."

"Patience, milady. Every miracle needs a little more perseverance."

Nev handed her the empty glass, making her pour the water from one glass into the other and urged her to drink. Watching Tessa sip her last drop of water, Nev smiled proudly.

"It's done.". he said, raising his thumb, then laughing out loud.

"Lipstick?" Tessa asked, shortly touching her lips.

"Lipstick." he nodded.

●

Tessa was now standing in front of the door, feeling ready for the red carpet. Nev's presence wasn't negligible either. From outside, Ruby began to unlock the front door. Tessa opened it for her in a rush, before she even managed to properly turn the key.

"Oh!" Ruby breathed in surprise, not knowing if it was Tessa's outfit or Nev's presence. She did, in fact, not know who he was.

"Hey, Ruby. This is my friend, Nev."

Nev tilted his head.

"Pleased to meet you."

"And we're just leaving."

"Oh, okay," Ruby murmured, pulling the key out of the door she hadn't been able to unlock. "Where are you going?"

"To the wild east: Hackney Wick." Nev said.

"Dressed like that?"

"There's a dress code."

"Anyway, see you later tonight." Tessa said to Ruby before making way for her to her own apartment.

As Tessa and Nev turned towards the main street, Raresh grabbed Ruby's door before it closed.

"Hi, Ruby." he greeted her kindly.

Ruby turned towards him in surprise.

"Wow, what did my house turn into? A tube station?" she murmured, rather irritated.

Raresh paused before speaking.

"I was thinking maybe you'd like to go out for some fried chicken?"

"I still find it weird that you bump into me this often." She looked over his shoulder to see if he had brought his car. "But I know we're neighbours."

"I walked here, yeah. So, are we going?"

"No." she cut him off, grumpy but flattered at the same time. "Is fried chicken all you have all day long? Besides, I had a bad day. And I don't like the fact that you're assuming that I'm available anytime you want me to."

Raresh stepped back immediately, putting his hands in his jacket pocket.

"Ruby, I like you. My insistence comes from a place of sincerity, which I assumed we shared. But I hold on to the idea that in a relationship, both sides have to meet halfway. Have a good afternoon, Ruby." he added, then turned his back on her and headed home.

She stood in the doorway, still holding the doorknob until Raresh disappeared from her view.

●

"Welcome to Hackney Wick!" Nev exclaimed, with both arms raised and gravity in his speech. "We've arrived twenty minutes early for being thirty minutes early. More than perfect." he added, looking at his wristwatch.

Immediately, it started raining. The streets were cleaned of all the dust. Less so the dust and graffiti. Those remained intact.

"We better hurry." he added, offering Tessa his arm.

"I don't think I've got anything to do with this place," said Tessa, as they both stepped into a rather artsy looking room. "I've got nothing to show."

"Yes, you do. Choose a job, milady, and wear it with pride."

"But I've got no experience. I don't know what I'm talking about."

"And? You are whoever you want to be. Then you say whatever nonsense goes through your mind. And voilà. It's that simple." Nev grinned.

The bouncer approached them to ask for the entrance tickets.

“We just want to use the toilet.” Nev said confidently.

Without any complications, the bouncer pointed at the corridor to his right.

“Simple, milady.” Nev whispered as he led Tessa in that direction.

A painting of Jesus was displayed near the ladies restroom.

“Look who's showing us the way.” Nev chuckled, taking out his e-cigarette and inhaling some smoke. He then hurried Tessa to the main hall, where the event was taking place.

Remixed '40s music blasted from all the speakers. Nev seemed in his element. A crowd of hippies was huddled in the concrete hall, with drinks in their hands and having to shout to make themselves heard. Their outfits were all over the place. Some looked elegant and conservative, others were rather nude and bold.

“Have I ever told you, milady, that on the night I was born, it only played 40's music on the radio?”

“Could it be related to the decade in which you were born in a previous life?”

“Oh, milady, I'm a '90s baby. But at heart, I’ll always be a traditionalist,” he said, still having a reluctance to reveal his exact age. “So, who knows?”

Tessa wasn’t sure what was bothering her the most. A few hipsters walked towards them.

“You’re a director of photography.” Nev whispered.

“I am, what?”

“If you don't know what to say, just change the subject.”

“Why would I do that?”

“And if someone asks you where we met, you say at a party.”

“Why a party?”

“It's always good to put it that way.”

“I’m nervous.”

“For what? It's a room full of people who’re obsessively watching shows that tell them when to laugh. You don't have to worry, milady.”

The first individual hugged Nev with a sigh. Tessa stepped aside.

“I haven't seen you in a century!” she exclaimed, finally letting go of her insistent grip.

"I know, right? Let me introduce you to Tessa. Tessa, this is Vanessa, our *Vogue* cover girl."

"Oh, where are my manners?" she commented, approaching Tessa to give her a hug as well.

"*Vogue*!" appreciated Tessa. "Which number?"

"Oh, I was considered for the cover once. By my photographer neighbour, who shot a few covers and who knows a person or two in that enclosure. But in the end, another model was hired. One with a portfolio."

"With a bigger portfolio than yours?" Tessa asked.

"No. With a portfolio."

Tessa scratched the back of her neck. Nev was already in the middle of another discussion near the snack bar. Vanessa also disappeared and a new individual appeared next to Tessa, introducing as Lucas. Lucas was also an actor.

"And what productions have you worked on, Lucas?" Tessa tried to make conversation, since he seemed relatively friendly.

"Excuse me, what?" he shouted, to be heard on top of the deafening music.

"What movies can I see you in?"

"None."

"Oh."

"I've always wanted to see myself on the big screen! So I decided to fulfill my dream and call myself an actor."

"But don't you have to be in some sort of production before you can call yourself an actor?"

Lucas was now distracted by a passerby who opened his can of beer before joining a group by the front door. Lucas's attention returned as he rotated his gaze like a turtle.

"Yes, so… So… Sorry, where was I?"

"Don't you have to appear somewhere before you can call yourself an actor?" Tessa shouted.

"No, not necessarily. But it's complicated. It's complicated, you know, because that's the way it is in this industry. Complicated. Do you understand what I mean?"

"I think so?"

"But how about you? What's your occupation?"

"Uhm, I'm not part of this industry." Tessa admitted after a moment's hesitation.

Lucas was now distracted by the toilet door that opened and closed every time someone crossed the threshold. Then, slowly, he returned to Tessa.

“Yeah, cool. Sounds good, man. I appreciate it.” he muttered, nodding a few times. “Sorry, what were we talking about?”

“You’ve asked me about my career path.”

“Ah, yes. So what do you do?”

“I'm a director of photography.”

“That's life, my friend. You know what I mean?” he smiled wistfully.

Tessa opened her mouth to speak, but then Lucas's attention shifted to a chocolate wrapper brought to his feet by the wind.

“Cool.” he smiled, nodding.

“I think I’m needed.” Tessa concluded, escaping in Nev's direction.

“Tessa, let me introduce you. These are Jade and Jack.” he pointed to an elegant couple. “The two are newlyweds and also work together as producers.”

“Nice to meet you, Tessa.” the two spoke.

“Likewise.” she replied.

“What do you do?” Jade asked.

“I'm a director of photography.” Tessa smiled, now convinced. “You two look great together. Where did you meet?”

“Thank you,” Jack replied, adjusting his sleeve to reveal his expensive watch. “At a party.”

Tessa looked at Nev and he winked at her.

“Are you currently working on any project?” Tessa asked, genuinely curious.

“What brings you here?” Jack tossed words in Tessa's direction without giving her too much time to adjust during the conversation.

Over Nev's shoulder, Tessa saw a familiar figure. It was Vince Charming, gripping a martini with one hand and leaning casually with the other. As Tessa's eyes widened and she tried to avoid looking at him, he noticed her and hurried immediately towards her.

“Uhm, I think we should go.” Tessa murmured.

“Huh?” Nev wondered, not knowing what was going on.

Vincent stopped face to face with Tessa. She began to squeeze a forced smile. Time stood still as Vincent moved his lips to say something. His movements were notably slow; so slow in fact, that Tessa was all the more unprepared when he vomited over her dress. As the vomit trickled over her shiny material, Tessa sought help in Nev's eyes. Swaying on his feet, Vincent leaned against the bar. All eyes were on them, and ironically, the music and neon lights stopped, due to a power outage.

"Oh, well. I think I deserved it." Tessa muttered, shrugging.

A partygoer tripped over a cable and spilled his whiskey over Nev's jacket. A microphone screeched.

●

Nev walked Tessa up to his favourite hill at Queen Elizabeth Olympic Park. There, the two sat on the humid grass. They faced a small street used by cyclists and families, even at that hour. Tessa had a damp spot where she had cleaned her dress. But it was drying out little by little with each breeze.

"You're baptised now," Nev said, taking off his jacket and putting it over her shoulders. "I could conclude that you were reborn, milady."

"You too. It smells like whiskey," she replied, gripping the jacket between her fingers. "Surely you want this back?"

"I'm too hot right now. It's yours, milady. Just like your decision to be anyone and whatever you want, as long as it brings you joy."

Tessa looked down the darkened alley.

"Now I realise," Tessa spoke after a long moment of silence. "I don't need anyone to make my life more colourful. I want someone to share his alcohol-soaked jacket with me on a cool evening." she smiled, feeling almost all her worries fading from her heart. "But why are we sitting here?" she continued, not understanding the purpose of the bushes and the mundane alley in front of them.

Nev promptly grabbed her by both shoulders and turned her to face the view at her back. Now the city lights flickered in the distance before her eyes. The hustle and bustle of the city that never slept intensified as soon as Tessa cared to listen to it. It was perspective.

CHAPTER THIRTEEN

There are many things we can't control. Our inevitable death, the weather perhaps, and the changes of heart occurring in those around us.

But what we can control, is the way we react.

Preached all the time. Easy to say.

Nev opened a notebook, where he had written down a whole column of names. He began to cross off the first ones.

Tessa walked through St James's Park with Mason, who tenderly took her hand and then asked if she wanted to go over to his place. Tessa stood still for a moment. Then smiled. Alex had a collection of sports trophies arranged on his bedroom shelf. Joseph was a book collector. Elias frequented a cafe in Tottenham Court Road.

Tessa helped Nev cross off the next names in their inventory as brown leaves began to fall and the wind heralded a hard winter ahead.

Nolan talked a lot, but without making real conversation. Tessa didn't mind, because she knew they wouldn't see each other a second time anyway. Aaron hated candy and she couldn't remember Ian for more than that he liked to wear two scarves at the same time.

Nev helped Tessa flip through the diary.

"What do you like to eat, Mike?" Tessa asked.

"My name is Oscar," he replied. "And I'm a cook. Want to try one of my recipes?"

Tessa supplemented additional information to the notebook. Nev rested his elbows on the back of the bench they were sat on and admired the ever-changing nature.

Along with Nash, Tessa stepped into a bar in Piccadilly Circus, immediately recognising the tables at the entrance.

"Oh, I was here the day before yesterday!" she exclaimed excitedly.

"For the business meeting you told me about?"

Tessa looked for Nash to see what he was talking about.

"Yes..." she agreed then, forcing a smile.

•

Several scurrying pigeons flew towards the clouds in Trafalgar Square. Tessa climbed into a high bar chair, face to face with Ruby.

"I don't know. It's as if all the companies I want to work for don't want me. And the ones I don't want to hear from, they call me every day." Ruby sighed.

"Sounds familiar. But yeah, no good company called me either."

"But guys are calling, ain't they?" Ruby grinned. "Tell me. How many people are you dating?"

"A few."

"A few?"

"Quite a bunch."

"Tessa, I think you should focus on one person at a time."

"That's what I do. I pay more attention to myself." Tessa smiled, ordering two glasses of Long Island for herself. It was happy hour and she had no one to share the second glass with.

"I mean, it gives me the impression that you've changed."

"In what way?"

"I don't know. I don't know how to say it, but I don't think it's okay for rumours to spread that you're going out with several men at the same time. People might describe you as —"

"A slut?"

"Yeah."

"And how do you describe men going on dates?"

There was silence between the two. This stillness wasn't the first or the last time a woman had to put up with while in a similar situation.

"I'm sorry, Tessa. I didn't mean that. You're right. Go crazy! What the hell are we living for?"

Tessa smiled. Ruby ordered a beer.

"What time does the gentleman arrive?"

Tessa looked at her wristwatch.

"Half an hour."

"Okay, I'll drink my beer before making myself invisible. If you need me, I'll be somewhere nearby."

"Why don't you stay?" said Tessa then.

"What, on your date? No way! The men you like are usually short and nerdy. They're not my type."

"No, Ruby! Stay until I meet him, please. I don't have much social energy today and if he's weird, it'll take me a while to get rid of him."

"Sure, no problem. I'll stay here to see if he's hot."

"I wasn't exactly talking about that."

"And if he's a creep, I'll make sure I take you with me right away." Ruby added, skipping Tessa's reply. "If you like him, I'll let you have fun."

"Deal." Tessa approved.

"Raresh isn't looking for me anymore."

"Who?"

"The fried chicken dude… I mentioned him to you before, didn't I?"

"Uh, I think so? What happened?"

"You know, I actually don't really want to talk about it."

Three beers later on Ruby's side and here was Rei. He looked just like in the photos. Standing tall, he was wearing a grey coat that reached his knees. His hair was combed to the side and his hand was warm when he shook Tessa's. His voice was pleasant and confident. American, on top of it all. Ruby stared at him in reverence, forgetting to introduce herself.

"Have you been here for a long time, girls?"

"About two hours." Tessa replied, sitting back on her chair.

Rei brought his own chair from the nearby table, placing it between the two. Tessa smiled at Ruby, hinting that everything was under control.

"I see you've had quite a few drinks already," he added. "But can I get you another round?"

"Sure. Beer, please." Ruby replied with no hesitancy.

Tessa touched Ruby's knee with the toe of her shoe.

"What?!" Ruby whispered to her as Rei looked for the waiter.

"Tessa, do you want a beer as well?" he asked.

"I'm okay, thanks."

"So, do you come here often? I don't think I've been to this place before." Rei added.

"I used to come here when I worked for my former company," said Ruby. "It was my refuge. Not too far out, not too local- either."

"I understand. What kind of job?"

"A call centre, nothing interesting, really." Ruby waved her hands.

Tessa hit her harder this time.

"How about you?"

"I work in finance. My company sent me here from Ohio."

"Fascinating!" Ruby exclaimed as the waiter approached them, bringing the drinks in no time.

Tessa looked at the phone Ruby was holding on the table. She took her own phone out and began typing. Rei emptied the first glass of whiskey in one shot.

"Why did you choose London?" Ruby added.

"He just told you his company sent him here!" Tessa replied instead.

Ruby's screen lit up as a message appeared right in front of Rei's eyes: *He's hot, you can go home now.*

"Oh! Oh! Where are my manners?" exclaimed Ruby, stumbling slightly before jumping off her chair. "I forgot I had something urgent to fix."

Rei laughed and Tessa rubbed her forehead.

"Are you okay? Do you need anything?" Rei stood up.

"I need to go!" Ruby exclaimed, picking up her jacket and purse in one swoop, hurrying towards the bar, but then returning the next second. "Took the wrong way. This way! Was nice meeting you, Mr. from the United States. Tessa, see you later." she added and then disappeared, not before bumping into a few clients on the way out.

"She's got energy." noted Rei.

Tessa raised her eyebrows, forcing a smile.

"Yeah."

A few glasses later, Tessa picked up her purse.

"Rei, you're a wonderful person, but I think it's time to call it a day." she spoke and he approved of her words. "It's getting late."

"Of course."

Tessa called the waiter and got her card ready.

"I've just noticed Ruby forgot to pay." Tessa sighed, then laughed.

"No worries. I'll take care of it."

"You don't have to. She's my friend."

The waiter approached and Rei grabbed the bill from his tray. He whispered something to the waiter, then brought his credit card closer to the machine.

"What are you two planning over there?" Tessa tried to get involved.

Rei smiled. The waiter handed Tessa his device, which showed three pounds.

"Service charge," said Rei. "Don't feel left out."

Tessa laughed and paid to end the evening on a positive note.

•

The platform at Charing Cross Station was surprisingly empty. Tessa was standing on the yellow line, staring at an ad on the wall. Trains were delayed.

An inexplicable sadness overwhelmed her. The thought that she was now endangering her own life by crossing that line didn't bother her anymore. She knew she had her life under control. All the decisions she was making were hers. She had the freedom to be her own boss in at least one field. She had gained this independence on her own. The uncertainties that once bothered her no longer existed. Instead, they were replaced by a void. A nothing, that didn't bring any joy.

A homeless man sat on a bench behind her, bringing some bags with him. A stream of air announced the approach of a train.

“Don't stand so close to the edge, miss.” he raised his voice. “You’re not safe.”

Tessa watched him and listened to his words. Feeling the need for closure, she sat down next to him. The train stopped. The passengers got off and the signal announced the closing doors.

“Smile, miss.” said the man as the train left the station. “Nothing is as bad as it seems.”

Sighing, Tessa nodded in agreement.

“If she tells ya she loves ya, bro, don't believe her!” cried a passerby in a hurry, talking on the phone. ”If she tells ya she likes ya, then believe her. Never trust women! Take her to a nice date in town, but tell her: This bro likes ya, but this bro ain’t loving ya!”

The passer-by reached the stairs. The echo of his voice gradually faded, until there was silence again.

“When my son died of cancer, I thought the end was waiting for me.” the man spoke. “My house, my job, my family. They all left me while I was battling his illness. In the end, I lost him too.”

“I'm sorry to hear.” said Tessa, looking at him.

“It's all right, my dear. There will always be a warm underground station to soothe my soul. It's not as nice here as it’s on Bakerloo or Central, if you know what I'm saying, but comfortable enough.”

These words stole a laugh from Tessa, proving that nothing was forever. Not even the pain each of us feels at times.

The man smiled.

“Do you think it’ll rain today?”

Countless trains arrived and departed that night, but Tessa and the man continued their conversation. There on the warm platform, where no one was judging them.

CHAPTER FOURTEEN

Raindrops piled up in a few small potholes in Chinatown. Hurried steps sprinkled the drops in irregular directions. The glowing lanterns were reflected in the now light-coloured puddles. Tessa made her way down the crowded alley, stopping in front of *June Storm*. Water dripped from her wind-curled hair and her clothes hugged her coldly.

Nev stood leaning against the wall. As if he had been waiting for Tessa all this time. A clap of thunder sounded in the background, which was rare for London and especially for a late autumn. Tessa climbed the steps, where she was protected from the storm.

"I just had a revelation. A conversation that opened my eyes."

"Astonish me, milady." he smiled, sticking his back against the damp wall and pulling out his e-cigarette.

"Life doesn't always go according to plan. And there's nothing wrong with that. We're all somehow messed up and that's okay." she smiled with confidence. "Do you know what friendship is, Nev?"

Cigarette smoke evaporated in front of him. The rain didn't stop slapping Tessa on the shoulder.

"Do you know what love is, in all its forms?" she continued. "Because I believe that any relationship can start with a friendship, if both people are willing to try. I also think that a relationship can end with a friendship. Or in hatred. Or the two people may never know what could've happened if they listened to the urge of being together. Infinite possibilities, depending on what we're able to conceive in our imagination. As long as we're fulfilled with what we have. The Universe never dries up."

Nev hugged her without saying a word. Like a reward. That she had listened to him. That she had discovered the parallel Universe he kept telling her about.

"You deserve me and I deserve you." she said, still in his grip. "Let's hold onto each other and go through life like this. With city lights behind us. Musicians around us. Freedom above us. Fresh air in our lungs and heartbeats in our souls. Now more than ever, we belong together."

"Welcome, milady. Have a nice stay in your new Universe." he said, taking his hands off her arms.

A beggar was listening to their conversation, huddled in a corner of the street.

The next moment, Nev presented his cigarette to Tessa, urging her to hold it in her own hand. She listened and took a smoke. Nev smiled lovingly and slightly melancholic. His eyes were filled with hope, but his lips tired of life.

"If everything I've ever felt was a gentle wind, this is a storm." Tessa whispered as Nev grabbed her hand, kissing the back of her palm, as if for the last time.

"Goodbye, milady."

Gradual dizziness overwhelmed Tessa. As she tried to grasp reality, her senses disappeared.

Coming to her senses at Leicester Square Station, the heavy rain was still hitting the pavement. Tessa looked around, confused. Did she walk to the station all on her own? How did she get here? She couldn't remember. Passers-by pushed themselves by her to make their way to the entrance. Tessa ran back to Chinatown.

Arriving at *June Storm*, she struggled to open the wooden door. It seemed to be locked. Bringing a hand to her forehead, she examined the building. Despair grew in her chest as the wind picked up. It was the first time she had stood in front of a closed-door at *June Storm*. And it wasn't even that late. Right now, when she needed Nev the most. Tessa shook the door again. Nothing.

"Oh come on, please. Don't do this to me."

Tessa fidgeted from left to right, hoping to come up with an idea or at least see someone around that she knew. At least Colin. Or the reason why they had decided to close earlier. But no such news greeted her.

"Can I help you with anything, ma'am?" a voice then asked.

An elderly gentleman appeared from a stairwell, staring at Tessa. His long, white beard immediately reminded her somewhat of Christmas, but she tried not to be distracted by his appearance. She once again looked through the steamy glass of the front door.

"Who're you looking for?" the old man asked, as he closed the door he came out of.

"I was just wondering why *June Storm* is closed."

"What are you talking about?"

"And yes, I'm looking for someone. Do you know if the staff is still inside?"

"I haven't seen any in a while. I saw some workers this morning. But they won't open the store until next year. I'm sure of this. Come back next spring. Until then, you got some time to check the menu. Who knows, maybe you don't even like the food."

"I don't understand what you're saying. I'm talking about this pub." she said, pointing at the locked door.

The old man shook his head.

"There's no pub here. It used to be a traditional pharmacy, but now it's a restaurant."

"No, I'm pretty sure this place is a pub." said Tessa, almost laughing at the shattering emotion this conversation brought her.

"It never was. The building dates from 1685 and was privately owned. Was renovated in 1890 and rented for use as a restaurant. It was said that they had the best soup in the city. In the 1960's it had several different owners, who opened various pharmacies. There has never been a pub or bar here."

Tessa smiled politely, wanting to ignore the tumult of information thrown at her. She stepped back. The massive building was completely visible to her eyes now. The rain couldn't stop her from gazing at it. The old bricks suddenly seemed foreign to her. She noticed that the *June Storm* opening hours weren't written on the door anymore either. Nothing looked the same as before. Tessa was now standing in front of a foreign building on more than familiar ground. She stepped back once more, realising that the old man was right.

The ticking of a clock echoed in Tessa's subconscious. It seemed as if the Universe was right now placing her back in the reality she needed. To continue her life exactly as it had to be. As she was prepared to do. The parallel realities had merged, but the only detail that didn't overlap was *June Storm*. The place where all the Universal energy had been set in motion didn't even exist physically. Tessa walked away confused and disappointed. She ran to Leicester Square. The streets were the same. The cars were just as noisy. The city lights just as blinding. Agitated and noisy citizens. The rain was cold like every fall. Tessa didn't have an umbrella. And Nev was nowhere to be found. Instead, miraculously, Tom crossed her path. He was wearing the same clothes she had met him in. His gaze was just as friendly. Tessa lunged at him and clung to his shoulder.

Lightning struck behind the two, as Tessa saw herself holding his hand. But then it was Dean, who smiled back at her. All of a sudden, dozens of images overlapped, showing Tessa countless possibilities and missed opportunities. All of those, which created her present.

She snapped back to actuality.

"Tom! We haven't seen each other in ages!"

He tilted his umbrella to look at her. At least he stopped walking.

"Sorry?"

"I'm sorry I misled you. I should've been clearer with you. I'm glad I can tell you that now. Your sincerity flattered me and I hope we can stay friends. Maybe we'll visit the cemetery together again someday." she laughed. "I felt lonely when I met you and I didn't want to lose you. But I gave you false hopes."

"Excuse me, do we know each other?" he said, which made Tessa take a step back.

"We went out together last summer."

Tom shook his head.

"You might mistake me with somebody else. I've been married for two years." he added, revealing an elegant lady standing beside him under his umbrella.

Thunder echoed again. As the two continued on their way, Tom walked as fast as he always used to. Tessa found herself in the middle of a familiar city, and yet so strange.

The gentleman who usually handed out the Metro at St. Paul's greeted her, handing her what appeared to be a voucher. He then merged into the crowd.

June Storm is a woman, said the note Tessa was holding between her fingers. Raindrops began to wash away the ink. Tessa picked up her phone and tried to log in to the app. But it no longer existed on her phone.

Passers-by appeared to get on with their lives as they would on any other day. Their voices gradually faded as Tessa looked around.

And thus, November and December raindrops sprinkled away…

CHAPTER FIFTEEN

December

Raresh was listening to vintage Christmas songs as he drove through the night. The snow was getting heavier as the car's headlights revealed a section of the road at a time. The cold wind blew through his slightly open window. Pulling to the right, he retreated to a gas station. He left his headlights on as he headed for the entrance.

Ruby got off a bus, running through the snow to the same gas station. There, Raresh met her eager gaze. He glanced around.

"What are you doing here?!"

"I thought it was time for us to meet halfway," she said. "I've brought fried chicken!" she raised the bag she was holding. "It's probably cold, but I think the intention always matters."

Raresh hesitated for a moment.

"How did you know I'm here?"

"I asked your neighbours."

"Oh. So the urgency for which Patricia made me stop at this gas station doesn't really exist."

"Who's Patricia?!"

"Ruby, the neighbour you talked to."

"Kidding." she laughed and Raresh took another second to get back to the previous topic. "So, do you wanna eat?"

"There will always be a free seat for you in my car."

Ruby smiled in relief.

"And I'm sorry. For everything I've said and for everything I've made you feel." she added, still hugging the bag of food, the oil of which was slowly dripping down her jacket.

"I'll accept half of your excuse," Raresh replied. "I'm not sorry you made me adore you."

Raresh hugged her, squeezing the fried chicken between their bodies.

"How nice to be around you. There is nothing better in this world!" Ruby whispered, unable to contain her smile. "I was mad for you from the very first moment I saw you. I just didn't know. Now I'm sure I'll love you for the rest of your life. But please, no pressure!"

"My toes are frozen."

"Mine too," she replied, though not intending to move too soon. "Can I please sit in the driver's seat while we eat? No big deal, but when I'm excited I sweat under my right armpit, and I don't want to make you suffer."

"Oh, I didn't know that."

"You have a lot to learn about me. But I promise, all just good things."

CHAPTER SIXTEEN

Thick snow. A white Christmas was looming in a merry London.

"Bro, bro! It's behind you! He's attacking us! Come on! In my opinion, we can win this game!" cried Imo, who had an entire attic at his disposal to unfold.

One level down, Ruby spread her make-up all over the table next to the mirror. Tessa had settled into the next room to be as far away as possible from Imo, who had now decided to play more consistently at night.

The office where Tessa and Ruby worked was packed with garlands and wrapped gifts. Ruby was busy at the computer by the window, sending Raresh hearts. The team behind her was gathered around a single desk, as they were choosing photos for their next campaign.

"Ew! I think there's vomit in the toilet!" complained Rebecca as she walked into the room.

"I threw my smoothie into that sink. Sorry." Ruby spoke without turning to her.

"What the hell was in it?!"

"Uhm. Bananas, matcha, yoghurt..."

"Okay, thanks a lot! It's exactly what I wanted to hear."

Ruby sighed.

"Have you heard about Fiona?" Rebecca then said.

"Hear what?"

"She's got an awesome new job in a bank apparently." Rebecca stood almost expressionless. "Can you imagine? Her, in a bank?"

"Yes, I can." Ruby said, firmly. "And I think you should let it go. You've been rude to her for no real reason."

Rebecca stood in silence, not being defensive this time, but reflecting over her words.

The other colleagues were still flipping through pictures.

Tessa sat on the edge of her desk, holding a hot tea mug in both hands. The snug steam warmed her cheeks. She smiled, knowing that there were many more layers to this mystery that was the Universe. She knew that the experience she had had was real. But even more certain was that she was heading in the right direction. Towards a life filled with abundance. Everything that ever mattered.

However, Tessa decided to never talk about her *June Storm* experience ever again.

She lifted her phone, staring at the job ad she'd been obsessing over for a while. Freelance photographers were needed. She just discovered her new passion.

●

"I love you *this* much!" exclaimed a young woman, standing with both arms wide open.

"You mean, like, 180°? There are bigger angles than this one, you know that, right?" Brandon spoke, his hands in his trousers, while the young woman pouted.

Some things never changed. What changed, was the way we looked and reacted when prompted.

Easy to say, as we'd established.

Citizens were crossing the Richmond bus station, leaving deep footprints in the snow cover. Nev burst out of a bar. Stepping into the street, he almost stumbled. With trembling hands, he looked for a cigarette in his pocket. He wore a black hat and a thick coat, but his nails were blue from the cold. His lips trembled, not just from the shiver. He placed his cigarette between his lips and pressed the lighter repeatedly, trying unsuccessfully to light it. The cigarette fell into the snow. When motioning to pick it up, he noticed Tessa, who was getting on a bus not far from where he was standing. A faint smile appeared on his face.

Tessa paid for the trip with her card and then limped to the back seats, where several students slept with their heads propped against the window. The driver was ordered to wait at the station for a while.

Tessa turned her camera on, leafing through the awful pictures she had just taken. "Wildlife in London" was the theme of her interview portfolio. Maybe they actually meant the city. She was unable to imagine how she had failed to such an extreme. Only the thought itself made her burst out laughing. She had run after deer across the whole park, just to be then chased by deer all the way back. In conclusion, her photos were awful.

She then noticed a young man out of the corner of her eye. He saw her as well and stood up, urging her to take a seat next to him by the window. She thanked him and sat down. He was occupying almost a chair and a half with his broad shoulders. Tessa covered her bruised knee with her wet bag, waiting patiently for the bus to take her closer to home. The young man was wearing a second-hand leather jacket that was way too thin for the weather outside. He took his phone out of his chest pocket and searched for his photo album. For no reason, Tessa paid discreetly close attention. He looked through some pictures of landscapes, snow, and deer. Tessa couldn't help but notice the clarity of these images and the perfection with which they would fit into her portfolio. She took a deep breath with almost obsessive enthusiasm. She then turned to look at the young man to her left. He noticed her intention. The deer disappeared from Tessa's mind for a long moment to come. The two's shoulders were glued together and Tessa realised she didn't want to be anywhere else in the Universe, except where she was now.

"Is everything okay?" he asked, alluding to the rather obvious wound Tessa was trying to hide under her bag. His British accent immediately stood out.

Tessa smiled. Not only did the bus halt now, but the whole world stopped to celebrate this moment. Tessa didn't even try to hide her momentary gleam. Like any researcher who had just made a great discovery, she too wanted to celebrate her success.

"You have deer pictures!"

"Well noticed. And you look like you had an accident."

"Are they real deer?" she hurried to ask.

"Are there any fake deer? I don't know, they looked pretty real to me when I took the photos."

Tessa giggled, and before she could even ask, she knew he was going to teach her how he took the photos. Tessa also knew that he would make her smile every day, starting with the uncontrollable smile she put on when she looked at him for the first time. Tessa knew that she would visit deer with him countless times, as well as thousands of other unknown and thrilling places. Tessa also knew that he liked to walk closer to the road, to keep her on the safe side next to him. That he liked long walks and that it was natural for him to walk fast. That he was never late and that he always arrived too early for any meeting. That he liked beer. He hated vinegar crisps. And that he would let her eat her chocolates filled with jam in the middle just the way she wanted. That he would give her flowers for no reason. That he would snore during boring movies. That he couldn't stand people who went to bed without showering. That he could play the guitar. And that he would make her cry of happiness on New Year's Day. She knew that they were going to unintentionally synchronise their steps while walking together.

And that he was the guy she wanted to spend the rest of her days with. Tessa knew, because she knew. Meeting him on the bus was more than a marriage proposal in December. It was the whole future in an instant.

Nev picked up his cannabis cigarette as Tessa's bus departed. He managed to light the fire and take a first and last puff. He looked melancholically at the back window of the bus, where Tessa's figure could be seen. The cigarette fell from his hand and immediately went out into the snow. Nev then decided to step forward. Since he couldn't stand properly on his feet, the passers-by avoided him while frowning. With one hand in his pocket, Nev struggled to mimic the ideal citizen that brought no trouble. At his next step, he collided with a pole which caused him to lift his hat.

"My apologies, miss." he said, after a short bow, then minded his way again.

His iconic laughter echoed across the street. Stumbling, he fell to his knees. Pedestrians walked around him, avoiding eye contact. Nev laid on his back with his arms wide open. Looking up at the gray sky, he noticed that snowflakes began to fall smoothly, closer and closer.

"That day is today." he said, smiling at the cold flakes that touched his face. "Neville, deceased on a cold December day." he whispered.

His gaze remained fixed on the sky. His features were as carefree as always and his smile was unmistakably present on his lips. But now his body was still. The snow continued to cover him and citizens rushed past him as the bus drifted away.

●

Sometimes we don't know what we want. At other times, we know exactly what we're looking for and we still mess up. But how can we anticipate what will happen if we don't face the future? Where can we find out if we don't let life happen?

Society is funny in a way that, from time to time, one-night stands lead to marriage. Long-term relationships end up shattered. Friends who like each other never admit it and some marriages are based on agendas over love. How can we ever know if we have made the right decision?

At the right time, we will simply just know.

•

June Storm is a woman. Free, strong, confident, messy, passionate, sometimes slightly tipsy. Cranky, confused, melancholic. At other times, loving, sincere, spontaneous. Happy. And always strong.

June Storm is friendshp. Loyalty. *June Storm* is mourning. Hope, healing, but also pain. *June Storm* are all those who are still struggling with addiction.

Bloopers

Through Jason's eyes

"No human being would say that!"

"'Truth that is' — What are you, Yoda?"

"Is he meant to sound dumb?"

"This isn't your actual point of view, is it?"

Edits sentence, makes it sound posh — *insert Winnie the Pooh meme here*

CPSIA information can be obtained
at www.ICGtesting.com
Printed in the USA
BVHW032038290123
657386BV00011B/205/J

9 781739 278618